MarsX

First edition published as a Kindle eBook, January MMXVII; This ebook and all its content may be copied and reproduced without author permission, (except that NASA images have restrictions).

Other works by the same author:

Life on Mars: *A Study of NASA's Mars Photos 2012*
Life on Mars 2: *Further Study of NASA's Mars Photos 2013*
Life on Mars 3: *More Study of NASA's Mars Photos 2013*

Possible future publications:

Rockpeople: *2021*
Moon Life: *2023*
Life on Mars 4: *2024*

MarsX

THE FIRST MANNED SPACECRAFT TO MARS

Michael G Hunter

To order additional copies of this book, contact:
Xlibris
844-714-8691
www.Xlibris.com
Orders@Xlibris.com
832628

"A camel is a horse designed by committee."

Sir Alexander Arnold Constantine Issigonis 1958

Contents

Introduction

This book is not just about space travel to Mars; it's about fighting preconceptions and thinking outside of the box, and getting to the truth. Anyone who has paid any attention to Mars has developed preconceptions about it. Scientists have guided our preconceptions and formed many of them with their consistent and well-published opinions and suppositions about the "dead" and "dry" "lifeless" planet, through science presentations, television science shows, movies, documentaries, news articles, books, and magazines as well as internet publications. Tests for life on Mars have not been overwhelmingly conclusive to scientists, and in spite of limited success, most scientists seem to agree that Mars has no life at all worth mentioning. A few have come to believe otherwise. Some believe there are, at best, microscopic life forms such as algae or microbes. A few have outwardly stated that they believe Mars has life, but without specifics. And a rare few, with ridicule ignorance from the broader scientific community, still claim to see life in the rover photos.

Preconceptions about Mars

The primary preconception about Mars, which is almost universal, amongst scientists and public, is that Mars has no life at all. This has been a scientific assumption that has been used for decades to educate people from childhood in the teachings of science in grade school, junior high school, and high school, and even in college science classes. Anyone with a formal education at any level has been conditioned to believe it. Simply put, in my opinion, the problem is visual. Our photographic processes somehow do not allow moving objects, including people, animals, and living things, to be seen clearly. Furthermore, the process of transmission of images over millions of miles does not capture the clarity of normal visual quality that most people need for conclusive interpretation of images. Therefore, scientists, without unquestionable evidence, do not accept that occasional images of things such as fish or animals or reptile or even people, scientists simply refuse to believe that they are anything but rocks.

Curiosity Rover Photo PIA17083

A second preconception about Mars is that there is no water, the planet is dry. This is not quite as widely believed as the life issue, but generally it is believed that water cannot exist for any duration on Mars without boiling off, evaporating. Some water has been observed from time to time in photos from satellites and rovers. But the general idea of water on Mars is that it is scarce and that supports the non-life theory. In fact, water does boil at 45 degrees Fahrenheit at the low atmospheric pressure of Mars. Therefore, when the water temperature gets above that temperature, it boils. However, the photos from Mars seem to indicate water, in puddles, pools, and in some cases, large lakes inside craters such as the landing crater of Curiosity rover. It probably remains below the temperature required to boil off, sometimes, but most of the time it is frozen, yet does appear to boil off at midday.

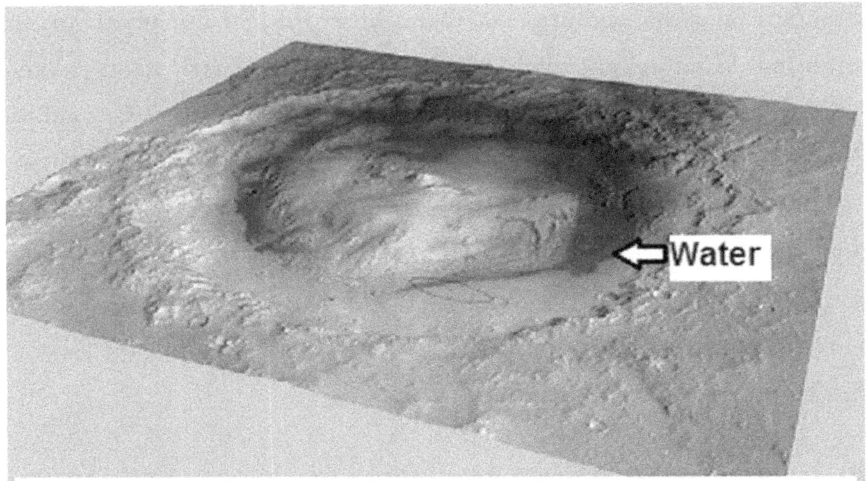

Gale Crater, Curiosity Rover Landing Site

A third, less common preconception regarding Mars is that it once had a civilization which has died out and all that remains is some ruins of their buildings and statues. Occasional photos seem to show such ruins and statues, partially covered or buried by drifting sand.

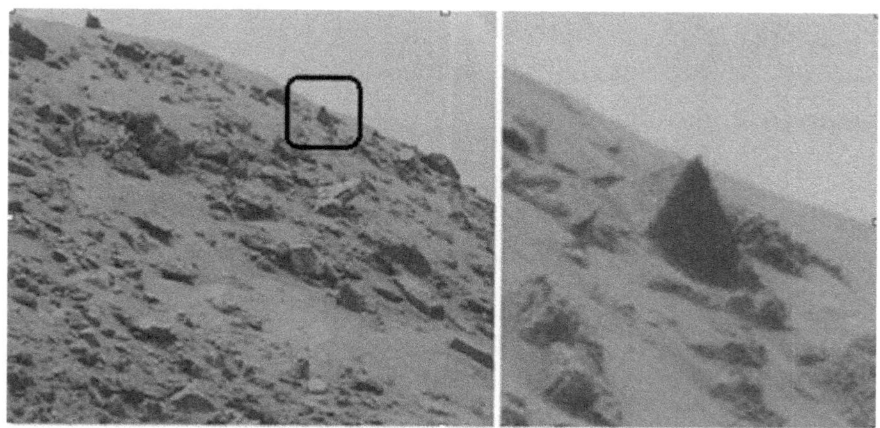

Curiosity Rover Photo Showing Pyramid on Mars

This preconception of a long ago, now vanished civilization, seems to be only among people who have studied the photos from a nonbiased viewpoint and seen the artifacts in blurry rover photos or highly enlarged satellite photos. In my opinion, this is possible, but I believe many of what look like statues are in fact living people, and the problem again is visual. The photography, as still pictures, does not allow us to judge motion and therefore we assume they are not living, hence, statues. The lack of color in the photos also tends to reinforce the illusion that the "statue" is made of stone, of a color similar to the stones around it.

Preconceptions About Aliens

Earthlings have many preconceptions, not only about Mars, but more generally, about aliens, (beings from other worlds), which they have gleaned from movies, television shows, and fiction writings.

1. They are usually thought of as larger than humans, or of similar size.

2. They are usually considered to be different in appearance, such as having fewer fingers, hairless bodies, large eyes, reptilian features, or insect features, or combinations of these..

3. They are thought of as being more advanced than humans in intelligence and technology, with craft that is more complex, powered by means beyond our knowledge, as big as a city or state.

4. They are thought of as being out to destroy or abuse humans, use them as slaves, or dissect them for research.

5. They are believed to be seeking resources for their own use, such as gold or uranium.

6. They know how to travel through time such as through wormholes, cutting travel time, thereby traveling what would take us thousands years at the speed of light, in short periods.

7. They know how to cloak their craft, making it invisible to us.

8. They have propulsion systems superior to ours, such as solar sails.

9. They have weapons that are far superior to ours, and they are so powerful, we are defenseless against them.

10. They come from star systems thousands of light years away.

11. Their planets have deteriorated to uselessness and that is why they are after ours.

Reality

The preconceptions above are, generally, just imaginary suppositions of scientists, science fiction writers and movie graphic artists. My studies of rover photos, Google Mars, and satellite photos have revealed that Mars has abundant living animals, plants, and people just like on Earth. There is water in craters and under the soil, much more than scientists are aware of. The possibility of ancient civilizations is something that needs to be studied after we get better observers, that is, astronaut explorers. As for the preconceptions about aliens, they are totally questionable, in my mind, until and unless I see otherwise. The beings on Mars are like us, in anatomy and behavior, although they differ from us by being of many sizes.

1

MISSION, CRAFT, AND CREW

MISSION

Mission Statement

"Go to Mars, live there, die there. Find and explore life on the planet. Find economic value that justifies future exploration. Record and report. Avoid any harm or damage to the planet." Louis Newcastle (Upon selection of final astronauts, January, 2026)

Funding

The "MarsX", aka "Mars Exploration" project was funded in 2025 by Louis Newcastle, a self-made billionaire, comparable to Howard Hughes. But unlike Hughes, Louis was not a loner or fanatic. He had friends, rich friends, who shared and supported his goal to reach Mars in his lifetime. So his many billionaire friends from all around the world, anonymous to avoid scrutiny, but strongly committed and hopeful for their moneys to make a difference, pitched in on this super-high-risk investment with potential extraordinary returns. Government funding of space research dried up as a result of a shifting of priorities due to many things: world disturbances such as global warming had caused storms, droughts, hurricanes, freezes, and flooding; armed conflict between western world and Iran, Iraq and Syria on one side of the world, and belligerent nuclear North Korea, backed by expansionist and opportunistic communist partners China and Russia, against fearful Asian enemies on the other, made the world seem headed for its seemingly destined destruction; NASA's reluctance to acknowledge life on Mars and the Moon, and the scientific community's denial on the subject, (despite photographs obviously showing humans and life forms in abundance on those two worlds); traffic congestion, housing unavailability, fuel shortages, food shortages, water crises, chemical spillages, ever more prevalent and resistant virus and bacterial diseases; people's frustration with their deteriorating lifestyles, racism, political favoritism, class warfare, and public organized protests. Governments pushed back space research as a diminishing priority, while government tax collection became inadequate and excessive borrowing, necessity. Interest rates skyrocketed globally, currencies devaluated at alarming rates, entire financial systems teetered on collapse, and economic statistics became uncontrollable. Public unemployment, inadequate income, and racial bias, all caused general dissatisfaction, led to street riots, anti-government, anti-war and anti-corruption protests, while food and water distribution lines, gas pump lines, and even private military groups caused massive frustration on regional scale. All of the problems and calamities caused space research to evaporate and migrate to private hands. Consequently, wealthy people, in a world where the wealthy became moreso, while the poor likewise got poorer, people from all sides quietly gathered and looked for relief in other worlds. Human life on Earth was disturbed. Escapism, anxiety, and survivalism were the prevalent way of life.

Simplicity Principle

Five billion dollars may seem like a lot of money, but a trip to Mars makes it seem like a pittance. As a consequence, the project from the beginning proceeded with low cost in mind. The MarsX project operates to the maximum extent possible on the simplicity principle. The general idea is to minimize wasteful expenditures, to achieve the objectives with minimal cost, to do what needs to be done with as little effort, personnel, materials, and redundancy as possible. This principle is implemented on every level, from the mission objectives, the design of the craft, the selection of the crew, the materials, method of propulsion, travel time, control of the craft, food and water, and essentially everything from a to z. The schedule was similarly tight. The only way to launch in the window of opportunity, with February, 2027 as the target, was to keep it simple. Louis Newcastle begged, borrowed, and stole, but he kept it within budget and on schedule.

The Landing Site

The landing spot was chosen just a month prior to liftoff. There was a huge meeting with all the scientists and their boss. Louis had asked them to pick a landing spot, and as it turned out, there was complete disagreement on the answer. Each of the 14 scientists in his employ had a different opinion, and the possibilities were all spotted on a map. Each of the scientists got up and presented his opinion and his rationale for his site. After three days of deliberation, when all of them were finished, they voted on it by a show of hands. They each voted for their own. So Louis, who had the position and honor of casting the deciding vote, then was in the awkward situation of determining the ultimate solution. He walked up to the map, then backed off a few steps, closed his eyes, turned around 360 degrees, and then held out his outstretched pointing finger and walked to the map. Where his finger hit the board became the landing spot. Having duly marked and identified the spot, each of the scientists, (who received annual salary of $300,000 on January 1 of each year, by a personal check signed by Louis), then proceeded to announce their support for the choice of the site, some of them even claiming it was superior to their own choice. The site, agreed upon with unanimity, was five miles west of Nipigon Crater (33:42 N Latitude, 81:54 W Longitude)... essentially the middle of nowhere, a spot where nothing is known. "Finally, we have a landing site. What's better for exploration than a place where we know nothing," concluded Louis as he adjourned the meeting on Friday afternoon.

Nipigon Crater, MarsX Landing Site

Route

The route to Mars was decidedly as short as possible to minimize the trip time and distance travelled. What is still considered the most efficient route, by mainstream science, the 'Hohmann Transfer Orbit', takes over seven months. That has been the accepted route for all the preceding Mars missions by NASA, India, and others, and was considered the "only" realistic route until Louis Newcastle asked his scientists in one of the early meetings, "Why not make the trip shorter...after all, isn't the shortest distance between two points a straight line?" His 14 scientists came up with an answer: they were able to cut that from seven months to only two months by leaving later, arriving sooner, and travelling faster. Rather than the seven months at 25,000 miles per hour, (175 million miles), the trip could be only 63 million miles and at average speed of 45,000 miles per hour. By reducing the travel time, they also reduced the amount of water and food needed during the trip, so the payload was smaller.

Furthermore, psychologically, two months, a long time for travel in itself, is much more doable from the astronauts' viewpoint. And the shorter duration allows less likelihood of things that could go wrong, giving Peter's Principle less time to act. The drawback? It requires massive power and delta-v, and uses a lot more rocket fuel. But for Louis Newcastle, in grand Howard Hughes style, the cost of fuel was unimportant. What mattered was the success of the mission, and that depended entirely on the success of the crew. A shorter trip meant fewer problems for the crew, and more likely success of the mission.

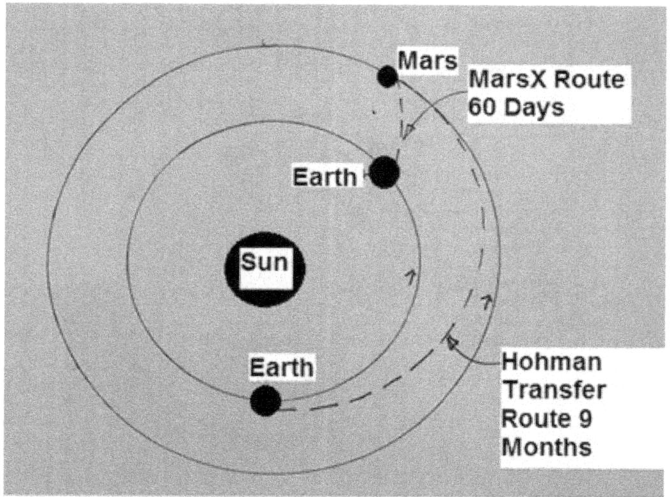

MarsX Route Compared to Hohman Transfer Route

CRAFT

The Mars X craft has three living sections: Control Room, Sleep Room, and R&R Room. On top of the control section is the 2-ton supply compartment, and on top of that, the descent parachute and landing gear. On the bottom, below the R&R, is the rocket, fuel, and landing gear. Insert Figure 1

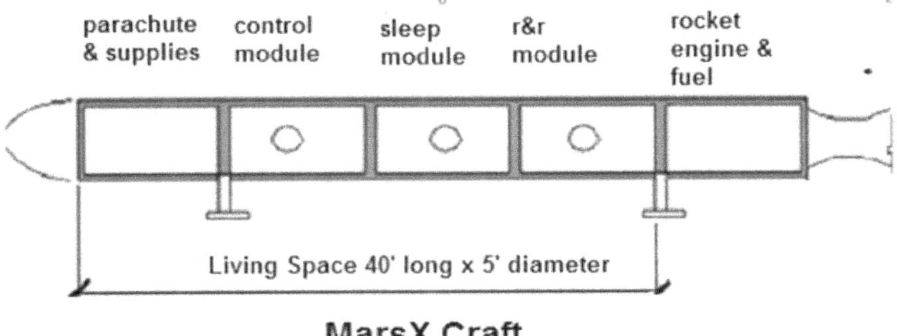

MarsX Craft

Tumble is for artificial gravity effect. By tumbling the craft at 2 rpm, end-over-end, the semblance of gravity is achieved at the control room and at the entertainment room. The central sleep section is gravity free. The simulation of gravity is necessary for us to avoid bone loss during the long voyage. Daily exercise helps also in that regard.

Exercise routine consists of one hour routine, daily. Routine includes weights, stretch straps, stationary bicycle, and treadmill. We hook up and can monitor cardiopulmonary data which is sent automatically to Control, where it is analyzed to study our physical conditioning. Blood chem is checked frequently.

Personal entertainment section consists of a 1/3 G (one-third of gravity on Earth's surface) gravity room where the astronauts can sit in an upholstered leather lounge chair, or lie on a comfy sofa with pillows, while watching movies, playing video games, listening to music, or reading books. There are snacks, like sugarless candy and juice bar. There's a coffee table, and a large monitor, sound system, and storage rack.

The travellers don't actually eat "food". They drink a mixture of nutrients, all the necessary glucose, vitamins, minerals, proteins, carbs. called "gluck" Everything is just drunk and swallowed, with no waste containers or leftover food. It's like the nutrient drink "Ensure" which anyone can drink on Earth. It dispenses from a tap into a canteen which we suck with a straw to keep the cabin air clean. Nobody wants to inhale gluck or water and we are all trained to keep the cabin as clean as possible. Since it is all liquid, they don't have to defecate. This reduces waste and also keep payload down. The gluck is piped from the supply module along with water, to R&R. For variety, there are several flavors, which can also be mixed: (vanilla, chocolate, strawberry, blueberry, grape, orange, etc,); the astronauts simply push a button, and get whatever they prefer, pressure-fed to canteens on their belts. It is made from egg whites, fruit and vegetable juices, soy milk, and other wonderful foods. It's a little like thin milkshakes.

Water and several juices are also available from the tap in the entertainment module, piped from the supply module. It's recycled in a superfilter worn on belts and replaced daily. Urination is into a catheter and that drains to the superfilter, eventually filtered and purified and goes back to our water canteens. This reduces waste and minimizes payload. Users only need to empty, rinse, sterilize, and refill the canteens once daily.

There's a small water closet, in R&R, but it's hardly used. It's only for emergencies, like motion sickness and to rid the interior of undesirables. It uses a solar powered heating element to dry the waste and the water is condensed and reused. There's a shower in R&R, which is a sealed compartment, which we can use any time. Water for the shower is superfiltered, purified, and then recycled to the supply tank. We disrobe, then enter, close the door, and push the spray button. It squirts water for about ten seconds at a time from several fine-spray nozzles. Astronauts get wet, soap up, rinse, and then blow dry in just a few minutes, using only about one gallon per shower.

Wastewater is then distilled, and recycled. Water supply is supposedly enough for a year, after which we need to eventually figure out how to make our own on Mars. Training delved on the knowhow and equipment to extract water from minerals on Mars.

The rotating camera is located at one of the viewing ports in the sleep section. Since the craft is tumbling at 50 rpm, looking out the window makes the travelers dizzy. So there is a telescopic camera on one side which can be set to rotate in the opposite direction at exactly the same rotational speed as the craft. Then that view is linked to monitors in each section, so a picture of Mars can be seen from anywhere in the craft. On one side the camera aligns to Mars; on the other side, a second camera aligns to Earth.

Hull consists of a gold-plated, 1/4" thick titanium-stainless steel skin over a 1/4" thick carbon fiber shell, which has polyisocyanurate insulation 1" thick inside that, and finally, a 1/4" thick molybdenum-stainless steel alloy for the inner walls. That is for the living quarters. The supply section and the rocket, fuel, oxygen, and landing section are 3/8" thick gold-plated titanium-stainless steel alloy over 1/2 inch thick carbon fiber. The gold plating helps with cosmic ray reduction, while the other materials add strength to resist meteor and space debris impact.

CREW AND GEAR

Because it was to be a one-way journey, it seemed appropriate to open the qualifications for crewmembers to those who were able to accept that. There were initially about 143 million applicants from around the world. After eliminating most through questionnaire and application information, one hundred final candidates were thoroughly analyzed through investigation and interrogation, and disqualified for the following: too big, too small, not speaking fluent English, having living spouses, close family, or lovers, having a record of criminal activity, abuse of drugs, health concerns such as lack of balance, poor hearing, poor vision, poor memory, missing extremities, psychological problems, cancer or other health difficulties, poor attendance records, poor attitude, intolerance, racial bias, religious bias, ethnic bias, social status bias. Through questionnaires and in the end, interrogation, the applicants were evaluated for likely reaction to abstinence from food, social activity, sexual activity, and family attachments. Finally, the number of candidates was down to 10, who were given intelligence and physical endurance and capability tests, such as vocabulary, general and scientific knowledge, 100 meter dash, one-mile run, shot put, and standing broad jump. In the end, three candidates and three alternates were chosen. The three-person crew that was selected by the scientists, by vote, consisted of two women and one man. This came after two weeks of evaluation and study, and is derived from the sitcom, "Three's Company", which was Louis Newcastles favorite situation comedy from his childhood. Although some alternates were older, the final three astronauts for the project were ultimately three sexagenerians. The names are not "real" names, but names applied during training. The astronauts received extensive hypnotherapy which altered them psychologically to prepare them for the trip for

Mars, including long term memory disablement. The long term memories were not eliminated entirely, but rather, were suppressed to the point where they could be retrieved only one way: by a secret code word known only to Louis Newcastle. This was to keep the possibility alive of reviving the memories in case the project came to an end unexpectedly before it's completion. The three crewmembers were chosen, as follows.

Sister Margie: Age 62, Japanese ancestry, about 4 feet, 3 inches tall, weighs around 90 pounds.

Sister Marsha: Age 65. African ancestry, scientist, is four feet 8 inches tall, 100 pounds.

Brother Mark: age 68, European ancestry, 4 feet 10 inches tall, weight 110 pounds.

As for the crew relationships, dozens of intense hypnotherapy sessions during training delved on that subject. The astronauts are, for all intents and purposes, "brother and sisters", working together on a common goal to which they are totally committed for the rest of their lives. They are even closer than real siblings in a family. They are friends and copartners in everything. They care for each other, help each other, and don't ever say or do anything harmful to one another. This is locked into their minds by hypnotherapy, and is reinforced weekly with dvd's containing subliminal persuasions.

Brother Mark, in a speech he had prepared for the prelaunch media meeting, the day prior to launch, explained much of the provisions for the trip well:

"We are one. We always refer to each other as Sisters Margie and Marsha, and Brother Mark. This is not just a matter of respect, but also it is a habit pattern we have ingrained into our minds. Also, any time we have psych problems, we solve them with hypno. There's a thirty minute CD in the r&r room for hypno-recharge. It recharges us and induces ultra-long-term memory amnesia, so we have essentially no sex or eating compulsions and we do not remember our former lives, prior to training. During our eight hour shifts, we are all essentially separated in the three compartments, but connected by speaker/microphones at all times. There's a door seal between each section so we can seal off a section if necessary. Any time someone says something, mumbles, burps, talks in our sleep, whatever, we all hear it. We see each other and high-five as we pass each other as we change shifts. Everything we do is on camera with multiple monitors and seen by ourselves as well as Control. There is no privacy except for the toilet and shower in one corner of the r&r section. The hypno helps us to cope with that, in training.

(Although the hypnotherapy was deemed by the project psychologists to be a necessity, to strengthen the astronauts' ability to endure the journey, it was highly debated by the other scientists, but in the end, Louis gave it the go-ahead on the condition that it was "undoable".)

Mark continued, "Our gear includes a light "space suit", (gesturing quotation marks with his fingers,) for use on Mars. The primary and most important part of the suit is a helmet which forms an airtight seal around the neck and allows pressurization to some extent. It isn't useful for spacewalks, that is, vacuum, but it is good enough for Mars. It's flexible plastic sheeting that has a pressure seal zipper like on ziplock bags which goes from the top center down to the back center. It has a viewport which wraps around the eyes and gives essentially 180 degree view. It's got a strap that goes around the neck and can be tightened by a belt. It has two orifices for air intake and outflow. A pressurized air cylinder is mounted on the back of the head, to give breathing air, similar to scuba gear but smaller. The idea is to use on a very limited basis, fifteen minutes at a time, on Mars, while most of the time the astronauts would be within the pressurized, airtight craft. It can work in space but is discouraged due to the high leak rate around the neck and the small air supply tank, which is good for only ten minutes."

Questions from the media were allowed after Mark spoke. The media questioned thoroughly but his answers were mostly beyond their understanding.

"What will you eat?" asked one reporter.

Mark explained that they would consume a nutrient drink during the flight, and that there would be enough for six months on the planet. "We believe, from rover photos, that there are growing plants and animals on Mars which are difficult to see in the rover photos. During training, we were shown many photos from the Curiosity rover which included primarily plant-eating animals such as rhinocerous, bighorn sheep, ducks, and even herbivorous dinosaurs like stegasaurus and brontosaurus. The large number of herbivorous animals suggest that, and even proves that, there is vast underground plant life on Mars. There are also many fish, living beneath the sand, including huge fish seen on Google Mars. Even a cob of corn has been seen on rover photos.

There are a large number of possible food sources which we will explore and report for future missions, as per our mission statement.

"What precisely is the mission of MarsX?" another reporter questioned.

Mark explained by quoting the mission statement verbatim: *"Find and explore life on the planet. Find economic value that justifies future exploration. Record and report. Avoid any harm or damage to the planet."*

Then, another question came: " So what kind of economic value could possibly justify future exploration?

Mark explained that, from careful rover photo analysis, it has been seen that there are many archeological items lying in the sands. It is believed that these things are from Earth. For example, there are gold coins lying on the surface of the sand. These coins appear to have Roman numerals on them, and that is why we believe them to be from Earth. Such coins would be worth millions, and actually, hundreds of millions of dollars, if returned to Earth and auctioned. There appear to be many other ancient archaeological treasures just lying in the sand, waiting to be retrieved. Here's a collection of coins from Curiosity rover photos. (An image appeared on the large monitor.) So that is one subject we will be exploring. But there are others, such as mining and precious stones.

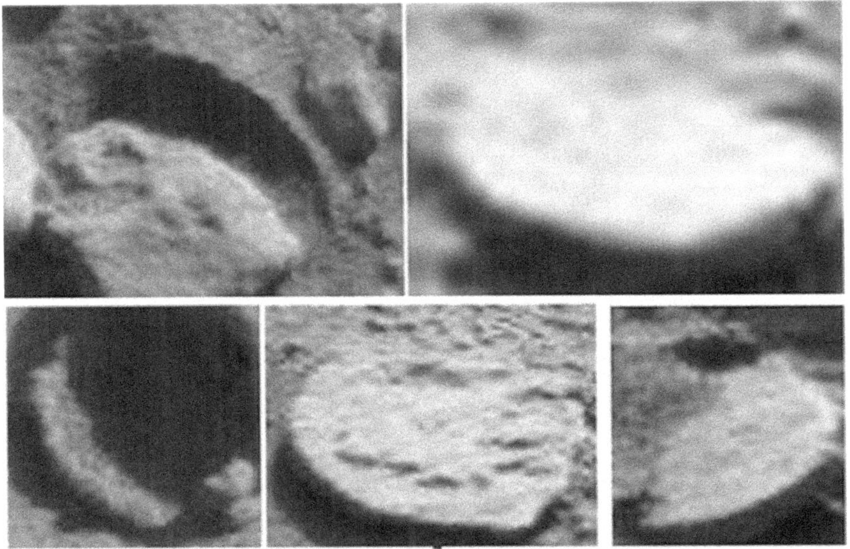

Coins in the Sands of Mars from NASA Curiosity Rover Photos

Louis Newcastle abruptly called an end to the meeting, explaining that the astronauts should rest thoroughly prior to liftoff the following day.

When the meeting was adjourned, the astronauts marched out of the room, leaving the press in disbelief, confusion, and awe, as dozens of reporters buzzed about what they had just heard

2

VOYAGE TO ARIES

The Astronauts' Logbook

Day 1 (December 21, 2026)

The vibrating thrust of the engines pushed us back into our recliners, and we could tell from the instruments, the pressure we sensed on our backs, and simply by looking out the portholes, that we were gaining altitude and accelerating. The steady roar of the engines and the vibrant shudder of the craft, our adrenaline flow, and rapid heartbeats lifted us to the stratosphere in minutes. We soon saw the curvature of the Earth. Launch had been smooth, problem-free, and soothing, like a bright sunrise, completely unlike the stressful simulation training we went through over the prior months. We looked at each other with smiles of relief, exhausted from going-away parties and celebration excitement the day and week before launch. However, as per training, our attention was focused, from the beginning, and continuously, on the monitors, gauges and needles, with occasional glances at the darkness of the portholes. Each of us, in accordance with prior scheduling, will sleep eight hours per 24 hour cycle, alternating with one person sleeping in the sleep center while a second works in the control section on command-communication and maintenance checks, and the third does exercise and entertainment in the R&R room. And, for safety sake, we work, sleep, and play in separate sealed-off compartments, just in case of some sort of mishap. That way two of us are always available and awake in case of emergencies, while one of us is always sleeping, or trying to. Every eight hours a buzzer sounds throughout the craft, and we trade places, a lot like musical chairs, high-fiving on our way through the sleep center to our next workstation position. We went several orbits, before maneuvering to our orbiting ion drive engines, so we were all prepared mentally to function well for that important maneuver.

Brother Mark

Day 2

With help from control, our craft was hooked to the ion drive engines. We turned on the rocket engines and blasted out of Earth's orbit on schedule as planned. We are headed for Mars! The ex-orbit burn worked perfectly. We all said our goodbyes to Earth and celebrated the start of our two-month voyage with a bottle of unwine, a nice burgundy flavored non-alcoholic drink made by The Grateful Dead in 1996, which Louis had been saving for over two decades for an occasion like this, and it was well worth the effort, as the taste was superb. We went through the bottle with ease and wished for more,

but we knew it was never going to happen again. Command gave us their blessings and wishes for a good trip. The craft accelerated from the orbit velocity of over 17,000 miles per hour, to beyond escape speed, over 25,000 mph, and after a thirty minute burn, we were cruising on our 63-million mile trip to Mars at 45,000 miles per hour.
Brother Mark

Day 3

Maintaining our cruise speed, if all goes well, for the next 57 days, we will arrive at our destination on the red planet on February 19, 2027, (the day of opposition). The Earth and Mars will be at their closest approach in hundreds of years. Although we are sitting in what resembles a giant gold-plated pen, streaking through the cosmos, it seems to us like we are standing still. The background classical music keeps the dead silence from being a bother. Nothing eventful occurred worth documenting on this day. We secured everything to prepare for the tumble, as planned, on day 4.
Brother Mark

Day 4

We began tumble during shift change, as Sister Margie applied the retros and monitored the rotation period to achieve partial gravity. After three days of weightlessness, artificial gravity felt good. Having an up and down makes things a lot easier and more normal, and we were all a lot happier in spirit. The only problem with the tumble, all of us agree, is that if we look out a porthole for more than a few seconds, we get dizzy, and so we don't do that, and focus on the monitors instead. We employed the rotating telescopic cameras to rotate precisely the same as our craft spin, and maneuvered the

craft for a view of Mars on one side and Earth on the other. This insures that our trajectory is in line, while also giving us a reference point so that we don't feel lost. Mars is still is just a little orange sphere like a beebee, on our monitors. Earth is like a big beach ball, slowly shrinking, not as we watch it, but hour-by-hour, we can tell the difference. Although we get some news from Earth daily, from Control, it doesn't amount to much. It seems about the same every day. North Korea fired a missile that came threateningly close to Hawaii. Vietnam protests China's expansion policies. Iraq car bombs happen pretty much daily. People die from tornadoes, hurricanes, earthquakes, plane crashes, and other things. But that's all behind us now, no longer a concern. Our mission is our concern. Our mission, for the rest of our lives, is Mars... surviving, exploring, learning, and establishing the groundwork for future Mars astronauts.
Brother Mark

Day 5

To help mask the dead silence, (when we don't play music), the speakers put out a sort of static sound, "white noise", almost unnoticeable, kind of like my tennitis. We play, at a fairly low amplification, various background sounds from the thousands of choices available, like elevator music, rock, most any country or beat music, natural sounds of waves, rain, wind, crowds, whatever we want. We tried them all and what we all seem to like most, and played most, was the "jungle" sound. So now, as the time passes, we get an occasional squawk or chirp of a bird or a monkey howl, and a rainforest downpour. During my r&r, I enjoyed "Total Recall"r.
Brother Mark

Day 6

No significant event occurred, worth recording. During r&r, I watched and enjoyed thoroughly, "Bad Ass Spider".

Day 7

We are all bored as hell after one week. Nothing much happens on a craft as it slips through the emptiness of space. We have started to assemble together in the control section on a regular basis for an hour prior to each shift. This is just a social get-together sort of thing that Sister Marsha, a multidiscipline scientist, with her sociology/psychology background, suggested we try temporarily. (Change or development of any kind helps to cut monotony of silent, relentlessly confining feeling during travel.) Of course we all know each other well, having trained together for months and being isolated most of the time during training from our relatives and friends. Also the hypno sessions we went through help us to accept the conditions, which most people would never even want to try. After trying the "social meeting" each session, every eight hours, we liked it and decided to continue the activity. It was helpful in many ways, not just for keeping us happy, but to make the trip more pleasant. Most of the time we are alone, by ourselves, separated from our compadres by walls of steel and airtight doors. But we are as one.
Brother Mark

Day 8

In our noon social meeting today, Captain Margie explained that she began having psych problems. We started out calling it homesickness, but then later we called it Earthsickness. It started on

Day 6, as I recall, but I didn't record it until now. This is actually the Captain's log, which Sister Margie reviews periodically, so I hesitated to put anything in the log about it until she gave me an okay. Today she said to go ahead and put it down in the log. Margie would be sitting in the play room watching a movie and we could hear her sobbing. At first we thought it was just some romance movie she was watching. But then it happened again a day later, and again each day. We discussed it in our shift meeting. What's it about? She wasn't talking at first, but later, Sister Marsha coaxed it out of her. It's all about regrets. As Sister Marsha says, we all have regrets about past decisions and actions. Even on Earth, every day, people have regrets. It's a normal thing to have regrets. They come and go. Nobody does exactly what they want to do. Don't worry about them. Just put them aside and carry on. We need to focus on our task at hand. That's what we all concluded. Margie agreed to do a hypno-recharge on her break. Hope it fixed her.
Brother Mark

Day 9

Sister Margie said "I'm fine. Put that in the log!" Nothing much else happened worth mentioning.
Brother Mark

Day 10

Ten days down, 50 to go! We are settled into our routines quite solidly. In our social meetings, (every 8 hours) we try to keep positive, talking about the ultimate landing and how exciting it will be when we get there. We know more-or-less what to expect, but not totally: desert, sand, rocks. Of course, we have been trained and hypno'd to be ready for unexpected, and to prepare for trouble, but in truth, just thinking about spending the rest of our lives on a sandy desert is downright difficult to think of in positive terms. So we joke about how maybe some day we will come across a field of gold nuggets or maybe some precious stones like diamonds or rubys or emeralds. Who knows, maybe we will find a pool of water with fish in it? Our imaginations get the better of us when we are actually, no ifs, ands, or buts about it, bored stiff.

Brother Mark

Day 11

Today we ran into our first significant meteor storm. We get hits every day, once every few hours, but this was different. We hear them, like grains of sand, "ping". This one was more than one, a whole bunch within a few seconds, ping, ping, ping, ping, ping. A rock the size of a pea that came clear through the outer wall and insulation, to the inside wall, and fortunately, did not penetrate the inner wall, although it could have, if it were a bit bigger or faster. I found a small bump in the stainless steel wall of the sleep section. I was sleeping and it woke me up, the "click" sound was across the craft from my bed. With the memories of the launch fading, and the landing on Mars far in the future, we tend to focus our thoughts and actions on survival. Our three major concerns are oxygen, water, and food. If a meteor penetrates a supply tank, it could cause losses of essential fluids into space, and threaten our ultimate survival. Of course the odds are low for that happening, but with a near penetration after only ten days, we have to worry. Suddenly the odds of a calamity seem more likely. Our speed at 42,000 mph is one factor; rocks and ice in space, an unknown hazard, is a second; 100,000 meteors bombard Earth's atmosphere every day. And of course the Earth's atmosphere acts like a shield for most of them, while we have only our hull. In fact, Earth itself is travelling around the Sun at a speed of 50,000 mph, even faster than our speed. So we worry more now about space rocks. Probability studies have shown that we might run into somewhere between ten and a thousand along the way.

Brother Mark

Day 12

Another meteor storm hit us. This time we weren't so lucky. A rock the size and shape of a pea penetrated the cabin. It missed Sister Margie by a foot. Sister Marsha was not so lucky. The meteor ricocheted around inside the cabin, hit Margie on the head, and fell to the floor. Prescious air in the craft started whooshing through the hole instantly. Sister Marsha attended to Sister Marsha while I pulled a stainless steel plate patch from the console drawer, detached the adhesive cover, and slammed it on the hole, all within about ten seconds, pretty much like training. Not much of our precious cabin air was lost. But Sister Marsha was knocked out by the space rock. A small stone the size of a pea had penetrated her skull and lodged inside her brain. As it turned out, she became comatose, and could not be awakened. Her heart beat steadily, and she breathed normally, but was unconscious. We could do little for her, but hooked up an intravenous feeder for food and water, strapped her in her bed, and waited. For hours we looked for a sign that she might wake up, but it didn't happen. The whole experience was terrifying and challenging! But we had survived.

Brother Mark

BACK HOME

Meanwhile, back home on Earth, our every moment was being tracked not only by Control but by half of the people on the blue planet. Our status was closely followed by everyone who had a phone or other media device.

It was similar to the Moon landing in 1969, and perhaps other newsy events such as the Lindbergh baby kidnapping in 1932, the Doctor Marilyn Sheppard's murder in 1954, and The JonBenet Ramsey killing in 1996. It was like the major mystery of the century.

We just got a bit of the feedback from Control about our worldly position, but we were considered "Heroes". The world paused from it's problems to follow us.

Day 13

Unlucky 13! Today we were hit again, this time was worse. At first it sounded like rain, as the myriad of sand and small stones grazed the craft. A cloud of hundreds or maybe thousands of sand- and gravel-sized ice meteors hit the ship and damaged it severely, all within a few seconds. Ka-bam! We lost our communications with Earth, one ice-meteor passing through the wall of the control section, and hitting the communications box. What was worse, was that we lost three of the four tanks for our water, half of our gluck, and two of our four air tanks. Control of the rockets seemed to flicker but was apparently working. We helmeted, and quickly patched the walls with 5 stainless steel patch-plates, and we were left with only 7 patches for the remainder of the trip, and that small quantity was beginning to worry us. Unfortunately, (or fortunately, depending on how you look at it), we were hit on our bodies in non-crucial places. I had a pea-sized ice- meteor like a bullet hit my right bicept, passing through the muscle but not hitting a bone, while Margie caught one the size of a poppyseed that grazed her rib cage, leaving a bruise, and Marsha, comatose still, had one, like a sand grain, bruise her right thigh after ricocheting from the wall. Seems like the big ones made a hole, and a few smaller ones found their way through the same opening, before we could plug it. Luckily, nothing vital was hit on any of us. The meteors were a mixture of sand and ice. The ice melted after a few minutes, eventually evaporating. While I patched my arm and we massaged our bruises, we had a meeting and assessed the situation carefully. With 47 days left before landing, things look bleak, even dire. Sister Margie, with one hand on her rib cage, studied the gauges and monitors for awhile and then gave us a report: "First, the good news. We no longer have communications with Control." (We all high fived, humorously, not that we didn't like Control, but we just have one less thing to worry about. After a second we realized the direness of the event.) "Now the bad. We lost half of our air, water, and food. Rocket fuel is okay. We discussed return to Earth. The situation was that we had only enough water and air to get to Mars, and nothing once we arrive. We had 4,104 pounds of rocket fuel. It actually takes 8,000 pounds of fuel, by Margies calcs, to return to Earth and land, and only 3,800 pounds to proceed to Mars and land there. Margie's assessment was that having enough rocket fuel for Earth descent was "impossible", while Mars was "reasonably possible". If we do get to Mars, the plan has always been to build up our oxygen by extracting chemically from rocks. Marsha knows how to do that with the equipment aboard, which is supposedly undamaged in the supply section. Sister Margie and I decided to venture on to Mars, and to continue our Mission, "Do or die, as per the mission statement."

Brother Mark

Day 14

After a day of recuperation, rest and recovery, we got together and discussed the trying situation in front of us. We decided to conserve our supplies by rationing them out over the remaining 46 days. By doing so, Sister Margie calculated, we would have just enough air, water and food to get to Mars, with maybe a bit to spare. After that we would find some way to survive by manufacturing oxygen from the soil or rocks, and possibly finding water and food, or we will simply die trying. As a consequence, we had to shut down the air supply and allow the air to get stale prior to purging it with fresh air. Food is limited to 500 calories per day per person. Water would be limited to a quart a day per person. We would minimize our daily exertions, including exercise, and try to be as conservative as possible with our activities.

At Mission Control, back on Earth, the loss of communications with the craft was seen as a dreadful occurrence. They could not know what had happened with any degree of certainty, without communication capability. Most of the scientists agreed that some kind of meteor impact or other unknown event knocked out the communications, as there was not much else that could have that effect. They did manage to see the craft on a monitor that was linked to an orbiting spy telescope, leased from the military, which was used to monitor the launch, orbit and ex-orbit. At the time of loss of communications, the craft was 12 million miles from Earth, so all they could see was a tiny yellow spot on the monitor that seemed to periodically change brightness every few seconds, an effect which was decidedly from the tumble. So they knew the ship was still on its planned trajectory, and all they could do was hope that the crew was alive. There was disagreement of beliefs among the scientists.

Three of the 14 scientists believed they had perished in a meteor collision of unknown size. Six scientists believed they were probably alive and proceeding with the mission. The remainder believed that more information was needed to conclude anything, and they refused to make any judgment at all unless communications were restored in some manner or there was some indication of the crew being alive. They discussed alternate methods of communication such as laser beam Morse code messages and sending a second communication facility with a catch-up rocket. No single solution seemed feasible to the degree necessary for implementation. Lois Newcastle began thinking about speeding up MarsX2. The second manned Mars spacecraft was scheduled for two years later, in 2020. He wondered if there was any way to hit the current Mars window. He arranged a meeting with his scientists.

Day 15

Having gone a day without an air purge, our oxygen content in the living quarters was down to half of normal. It's about the same as on the top of Mount Whitney, 14,500 ft elevation. We were uncomfortable, and started to have high altitude sickness symptoms, just headaches and mild nausea, so we purged the air. Our water shortage didn't bother us because of the recycling superfilter system on our belts. The food was subsistence level, but it didn't bother us much due to the fact that we were pretty sick of the gluck anyway and we all could stand to lose a few pounds. Sister Margie recalculated and figured we needed to cut further on our air use, or we wouldn't make it to Mars. We decided that we needed to make an assessment of the craft outer shell, so we prepared for an EVA, (Extra Vehicular Activity) which Sister Marsha was most practiced during training, but since she was still comatose, we decided that Sister Margie was the best to do that because she is the smallest, and more practiced than myself.

AT MISSION CONTROL

The meeting with Louis and his scientists was held early in the day. Launching Mars X2 within the current window was judged impossible. It would require too much to be accomplished in too little time, too costly to be affordable, and too much risk as there was too little time for cross-checking. However, a launch of a second communication facility was considered to be within program capability. Louis presented an idea: if shelved ICBM's, such as MIRV's could be obtained from the government at low cost, two or three of them could be purchased and brought together, and piggybacked as multiple stages, to launch a small payload such as a radio communication system. Conveniently, the training radio system for MarsX was sitting in storage, waiting for it's application two years later on MarsX2. It had been ordered, built, and shipped to MarsX to be used for practice by the astronauts during training. It was actually a working system that was planned for MarsX2 The scientists were asked to look at the possibility of launching within the current Earth-Mars launch window, and to report back within "a few days".

MEANWHILE

The news media all over Earth was reporting all kinds of speculation about what was going on. The little they could muster out of Control was that communications were temporarily lost. The craft was visible by telescope only and the craft appeared intact, but there was no way to know what was the situation with the crew. All kinds of headlines resulted: "Crew Lost in Space", "Crew Missing", "Mars Mission Gone", "Crew Alive?" etc.

The mysterious loss of communications was for the most part a stop in the heartbeat of the world, similar to the breathtaking event of Apollo 13 when it passed out of communication as it passed behind the Moon. The world held it's breath, desperate for any news on the Crew.

Day 16

Today we skipped the air purge, and Sister Margie did an EVA assessment of the outer shell. (Sister Marsha is still comatose but with heartbeats and breathing. We strapped her down to her cot so she would not float uncontrollably. She began to show slight signs of improvement by opening her eyes and moving her hands and fingers. I read about brain injuries in the computer in the Play Room. The best I could figure was that she had a hematoma, a broken blood vessel in the brain. A "subdural hematoma" is a brain hemorage inside the skull but outside the brain. All I could gather was that she needed to be treated somehow, but we had virtually no experience and no equipment or tools to operate with; no surgical equipment, no medicines other than aspirin, some bandages, rubbing alcohol, adhesive tape, gauze; that's about it.) We sealed off the control section, Sister Margie put on her helmet, and strapped it airtight around her neck. She opened up the door while I waited in the sleep room and communicated with her as she space-walked. When she exited the craft, Sister Margie saw that the outer skin of the craft was pockmarked with dents and scrapes from the ice-meteor storm. There were holes and dents on the Mars side of the craft, including holes that had been patched inside for the habitable portion of the craft, but also, holes in the supply section which of course were unpatchable. She returned, sealed the door, and repressurized the craft. Our plan forward was to gradually reduce the air pressure and oxygen we breathe to minimize consumption and prolong it's depletion. We conserved energy by extra sleep, reading, and lying still most of the time. We each did a few minutes of exercise instead of the usual half-hour or hour. By day's end, oxygen was at 9 percent of normal, equal to 18,000 ft elevation on Earth. We breathed heavily but otherwise, things seemed livable. We are still 44 days from Mars.

Day 17

Oxygen level fell to 8 percent before we purged. Again, we all had symptoms of high altitude sickness but after the purge, we felt better. Sister Marsha is still semi-unconscious, at least while she was not sleeping She seemed unable to speak with some unintelligible grunts and sounds, but could hear us talking to her and responded only by small movements and awkward facial expressions. I studied the computer in the play section again for awhile to try to understand better what she was going through and how to improve it. She apparently had a subdural hematoma, She could not speak, she could not walk or move about. She had confusion, headaches, amnesia and paralysis, and could not remember even her name or who we were or where she was or why. She knew nothing about the Mission or how she got where she is, on a trip to Mars. It was clear both intuitively and from my reading, that we had to remove the meteor from her brain as soon as possible but between the two of us, Margie and myself, we were just too doubtful of how to do it. We weren't about to do brain surgery. We were afraid to do anything but wait until we could develop a plan. I felt her skull with my finger and and felt sharp edges of the meteor under ger skin. It was near the surface. I tried to pick it out with my fingers but it was stuck, under a scab The idea occurred to me that, if it was an iron meteorite, I might be able to pull it out with a magnet. I decided to wait and think it over and talk to Margie about the idea. She agreed about the magnet idea.

The tiny orange dot has grown bigger. The blue dot, Earth, has gotten smaller. 43 days to Mars.

Day 18

No events. Air pressure and oxygen are 7% of normal.

****

Meanwhile, at Mission Control:

The scientists and Louis met again, and everything was positive. ICBM's were obtainable from the government at essentially no cost, (the government actually saved money by not having to destroy them). They could be piggybacked with some fairly inexpensive and readily-achievable modifications. The training radio system was working and available for deployment. Everything fit into the launch window provided the launch could be made within two months. The only problem was that it would not reach it's destination until after the MarsX flight had landed on Mars. The radio system would have to be landed on Mars very close to the same destination coordinates of MarsX. After a cursory check of finances, (half a billion dollars were taken from the MarsX2 account), Louis gave the go-ahead and work began. A radio system would bring communications back to the MarsX team soon after the landing, in about six months. Cost was minimal because the rockets were basically free and the radio was already purchased. The modifications and launch costs would be easily absorbed by the MarsX financial situation.

****

Day 19

Another lone pea-sized ice meteor hit and penetrated the R&R section. It was patched without incident. It seems that a thicker or stronger hull is needed on all parts of the ship, for future trips. A rock bigger than our patches might doom us, so we need some bigger patches just in case of that. Sister Margie patched the whistling opening immediately, while I searched the ship for more holes and checked pressure-tightness. We continued on our way. Sister Marsha, comatose, slept through it all. Air pressure and oxygen is down to 6% of normal, and we have no ill effects other than having to hyperventilate from time to time.

The problem with Marsha loomed heavily on me. I remembered that we had several refrigerator magnets on the door of the refrigerator in the Play Room. I collected them and then, wearing rubber gloves, and sterylizing the wound on Marsha's head with rubbing alcohol, put the magnets together and against her head and wiggled them back and forth for awhile. Lo and behold, the meteorite loosened and came out. But also she began to bleed from the wound profusely. This I expected, as I had read that she most likely had a subdural brain bleed and the blood had to drain or she could suffer permanent brain damage. It is necessary to let the blood out to avoid pressure buildup in the subdural cavity, the space between the skull and the brain itself. I put a sponge against her head and it absorbed the blood as it flowed out. This went on for awhile and eventually the bleeding slowed and stopped. With the meteor removed, and bleeding stopped, I felt relieved, I believed she may survive.

Day 20

No events. 40 days to Mars. Our journey is one-third complete. Cabin air pressure and oxygen is 5% of normal. The remaining solitary oxygen tank is now half full, insufficient for the remainder of the trip, hence, we need to reduce our oxygen even further or we'll never make it. Although we need to breathe more as the pressure goes lower, we seem to be healthy but lethargic. The name of the game is "don't do anything". Like mountain climbers, sherpas, and marathon runners,our bodies will gradually adapt naturally to lower oxygen levels by creating more red blood cells. We also need more drinking water under the lower pressure due to higher rate of aspiration, so we are reducing our use of shower water to make up for the increase in water usage. Originally, our showers took about three minutes, using several gallons. We now are down to a few squirts from a bottle and towel dry, just one prep and one rinse for each daily shower, using only about a quart of the precious liquid per shower each day. The water seems to evaporate within minutes into the cabin. Sister Margie says we need to reduce our food intake also, or we won't have enough for the entire trip. We're down to 400 calories per day per person now, and we are losing weight and getting scrawny. Sister Marsha is still semi-comatose as she has been for a week now. She is alive, and she is able to sip gluck and water once in awhile. Sister Marsha was the scientist. We are not brain surgeons, but we realize the rock has to come out and we discuss possibilities, (cabin tools), but are still fearful that we might cause irreparable damage. We just don't have the equipment nor the knowhow to do it. In the meantime we have our own survival to worry about.

Day 21

Hunger, thirst, heavy breathing due to thin air, and fear of meteors, all would normally amount to serious physical and mental exhaustion. We know that from training lessons, and as a consequence we are all trying to stay inactive most of the time. We sedate ourselves, including Marsha, with acetaminophen. We are essentially waiting for the trip to end. We count the days (39 to go)and remind ourselves all the time. But we are able to stay aware and alert most of the time, and we are able to keep up hope that we will make it to Mars, in spite of the bleak conditions. We keep reminding ourselves to stay calm, relax, and survive the journey. Meditation helps a lot, and we are spending most of each day meditating. Since the sleep section is weightless, it's ideal for depriving the senses. The best way to meditate is in a lotus position, with the body floating a few inches above the bed. To control drift, occasional light taps of our fingers on something solid puts us back to center. In fact, our training included meditation sessions, which turned out to be much more important than we had ever imagined. It is now key to our survival! With no communication, ship monitoring takes very little effort. We hardly have to "steer" the craft at all as it streaks through space in a beeline for Mars. Meteor impacts are our primary concern. We still rotate amongst our cabin sections, but now it's every 12 hours, while Marsha is out of the loop. We each try to do a bit of exercise each day, just to avoid atrophy. We noticed today that the little orange dot grew to 1/4" diameter on the monitor, while the little blue ball shrank to 1 inches diameter.

Cabin air is at 4% of normal. 39 days remaining. We are okay but seriously worried.

39 days to Mars.

Day 22

Meditation with controlled breathing is our way of life and our primary activity on MarX throughout our waketime hours. Each of us is gradually adapting to the lower air pressure, over time. We breathe in controlled fashion, taking in air, holding it, breathing out, holding, etc. We meditate at the control section while we work, at the r&r section when we relax, and in in the sleeping section also. The lower air pressure does not seem to affect us. It seems that due to the gradual reduction of pressure, our bodies have adapted. 38 days left on our journey to Mars.

Day 23

Although we try to avoid thinking during meditation, our minds wander, as events of the past and anticipation of the future keep coming up. Our training, our launch, the meteorite hit, all resound in our memories. The hopes that we will survive, fears of more meteor hits, and simple curiosity about our future on Mars likewise, keep sending us away from deep trance. We note them and move back to our meditative state, a state of nothingness, like the void of space itself.

During training they tried to prepare us for Mars. "It will be tough," they told us. "You will be challenged to your limits. You will find yourself in a world that is inhospitable. You will have to find some unknown ways to survive. The food will run out. You will need to grow food on Mars. You may find food there. We give you seeds to plant and grow. Your water will run out some day so you will have to extract it from the Mars environment. We give you enough for a six month period, what we think will provide sustenance, and it has been tested on Earth, but it has never been tested on Mars."

The meteor hit changed all that. We have barely enough water, air, and food to get to Mars, even with the strictest rationing. When we get there, we will have to find air, food, and water immediately.

Day 24

Our bodies have changed since leaving Earth. We are losing weight, becoming scrawny-looking and bony, almost like skeletons. We lost so far about ten percent of our weight since leaving, and on top of that, we have not been exercising as we should, to conserve air supply. Also our hair has grown out. We were all shaved bald at the beginning of the voyage, and now the growth of hair is noticeable. Our bare heads are all covered with grey hair about a half of an inch long. The objective is to not cut our hair during the entire trip because to do so introduces hazards to breathing in the craft. We strive to keep the air as clean as possible during the trip. It's too much trouble to contain the hairs while cutting, so the easy solution is not to cut it. We clip our nails carefully, making sure to retain all the clippings and put them in the waste bin. The women grow leg hair. I grow a beard and mustache. 36 days remaining to Mars.

Day 25

Since we have so little to do and we have little energy, having consumed minimal food and water, we meditate a lot. In meditating, the unexpected thought occurred to me that I could not remember anything prior to training. I remember things like writing and how to do things, but I simply do not know who I am. I can't remember my name, for example. I know, my name is "Brother Mark", but I cannot remember my last name. I can remember that about a month before liftoff, during training, I became Brother Mark. It eventually, after focusing on the question for several hours, dawned on me, through logic, that my memory had been blocked. They mentioned this during training, "blocking of memory is a vital necessity for the success of the voyage." I didn't know what it meant, at the time, and just forgot about it. But now, with all this time on my hands, I need to know, "Who am I?" I asked Sister Margie if she remembered her name before MarsX. She couldn't remember her last names or anything!. She didn't even know what I was talking about. "I'm Sister Margie." Was as far as I got. She must have thought I was losing my mind. But she also began to question her own memory.

Day 26

This question of who I am continues to bug the heck out of me. Sister Margie said "Hey, maybe we're just fictional characters in someone's imagination; we don't even exist." I thought about that for awhile, but I simply cannot, I refuse, to accept that explanation. I KNOW I was someone before I became Brother Mark, and I am determined to find out who I was previously. I don't know how, but I will keep trylng to figure it out. I continued to contemplate that question, for the entire r&r shift and into my sleep shift. I continuously tried to delve into my memory, but kept coming up blank.

34 days to Mars.

Day 27

I began to study this memory-loss or memory-block question, in my mind, almost full time, not only during meditation, but also during r&r shift, and during my control shift. I kept wondering "who am I?" over and over. I guess hypno, the probable cause of the amnesia, might help to unravel it. Also dreams. During deep sleep, I have dreams vaguely of other people and they are just flashes, images and seemingly memories, difficult to remember, but nothing really solid. But I think that with hypno I can try to remember my dreams. During r&r shift I use hypno to set my goals and review my attitude and determine my path for the near future. I simply add memory recall from dreams to that.

Day 28

Sister Margie also began to focus on the problem of our identities, since there was little else to do. She began doing what I was doing, using hypno and dreams to uncover her past. We were both doing it, almost full time, as there was little else to do but wait for the landing on Mars. We were beginning to focus on and remember our dreams, and we discussed them with each other, but they usually seemed vague and confusing.

Day 29

I remembered something. It wasn't exactly from a memory but a recurring dream. I remember a woman, a beautiful, familiar-looking woman, smiling and kissing me. I know that face from somewhere. Maybe it was a woman I knew before. But she is special, I know, I mean why would I only remember her, and often? We were close, very close, I know now, but I know little else about her.

31 days to Mars.

Day 30

I have more vivid flashbacks of the woman in my dreams and now I realize, she passed away years ago, a victim of cancer. I had a flashback in one dream,of her in a hospital bed, plastic tubes feeding her intravenously, dying, weakened and sickly, from the chemo treatments. I know she was a wonderful person, she must have been, since I remember her in only very good terms, and having remembered her just faintly now, I miss her and my past dearly. Other flashbacks brought me to believe that I once had an only daughter who also died, from some kind of virus. I could vaguely recall millions of people dying from the worldwide virus epidemic. We probably should not be thinking of these things, but my mention of these things to Sister Margie brought her to recall her own loved ones. Without Control monitoring us, and without our routine hypnotherapy, we realize now that we are beginning to become liberated from the mindsets we were programmed with during training, and we are again free to do as we please. Perhaps this could be called a revolutionary breakthrough in our minds.

Sister Margie talked about her husband and her daughter who had died in an automobile accident, many years ago. They were hit by a drunk driver in a head-on collision when driving home from a soccer tournament. She has a vivid image of them at the morgue.

Sister Margie remembered from early training discussions with Marsha that Marsha had also lost her loved ones, in a fire caused by homeless people in the building next door. Her husband and son were at the morgue when she returned from a business trip overseas.

So here we are, the three of us, streaking through the vastness of space on this trip to Mars. Knowing now that we have lost our loved ones brings us even closer, like family members, and explains to us how we fulfilled the project requirement that we have no immediate family members to beckon us home. The voyage, for that reason, seems almost therapeutic, in that it gives us more inner purpose where there was none, as if we were lost, prior to the journey. It's why we are here but also it explains our intense dedication to this one-way exploration journey. And, knowing our pasts, and remembering our loved ones,, helps us immeasurably in our mental well-being. We are greatly relieved and feel great comeraderie and dedication to our task.

30 days to Mars.

Day 31

Our voyage now is finally half complete, and we continue our trip with renewed enthusiasm. Today, we carefuly assessed our remaining fuel, breathing air, food and water. Our rocket fuel is intact, unaffected by the meteor storm, thanks to the extra titanium thickness of the outer shell. Our breathing air was cut in half, as two of the four compressed air cylinders were penetrated by meteors, causing them to lose their vapors in a few seconds. Since we had already used one cylinder, we have only a very limited quantity left, and so we need to reduce our air pressure, limit our purges, and keep activities to minimum. Water and food were similarly affected, and as of now, we have a little over one tank of each remaining. Had they been in single containers, we would probably not be alive today. We have just enough to get to Mars, as long as no more meteors hit us, and as long as we ration carefully. We believe, we will make it.

Day 35

I skipped entries in the journal for a few days. There was nothing to enter, and I was weak, lethargic. We were both sitting in lotus position on our wallbeds, meditating, waiting, waiting. O2 in cabin 2%. Food supply running out. At current rate food supply will run out in 22 days, three days before landing. With 25 days to Mars, water supply will run dry around the same time we arrive. It will be close.
Brother Mark.

Days 36-45

I recalled and meditated while focusing on the primary directives from training...five rules that were drilled into us a week prior to liftoff, which we were to obey without question once we landed.

"Do not harm living beings. Do not steal. Do not have sexual misconduct. Do not lie. Do not abuse drugs or alcohol."

These things I will not do when I get to Mars. We must make a good impression on the people of Mars. We must be good to ourselves. We must bring Sister Marsha back to consciousness and health. Brother Mark.

Day 46-51

O2 in cabin 2%, stable. Food and water supply dwindling. 15 days to Mars.

Day 52

O2 in cabin 1%. We are all emaciated, starving, dehydrated. We have barely enough food and water, at current rates of consumption, to make it to Mars. 8 days to Mars.

Day 59

We are approaching Mars. We are excited about it, and Margie and I are beginning to talk about it more. What was a little red dot is now the size of a basketball on the monitor. We can see the features on the surface like Valles Marineras. Tomorrow we will reach Mars, decelerate, and land. We are down to our last food and water, about one quart of gluck, and a few gallons of water. O2 in cabin is .5%. Sister Margie said the food supply tank is empty, after she drained it all into a two-quart container. That is all we have have to eat so we will have to find something on Mars immediately upon landing. We don't know what to do, the situation is so bleak we don't want to think or talk about it. We have water, a few days supply, perhaps. The guage is just above zero, indicating about three to five gallons We think we will make it to Mars, but then, our food and water will run out and we will have to find something there to eat, top priority. O2 in cabin .4%. We are all breathing heavily, passing into unconsciousness from time to time, but waking and able to talk to each other just to reassure ourselves that we are alive.

Mars on Approach by MarsX

3

LANDING ON MARS

The Astronauts' Logbook

Day 60/Sol 1(February 19, 2027)

Mars landing day, sixty days after liftoff from Earth!

We approached the planet; within 100,000 miles, we prepared for descent. With Marsha in her cot, still unconscious or asleep, Margie and I gathered in the control section and strapped ourselves to our seats. First step was to stop tumbling. Sister Margie used the retros to bring us back to a no-gravity, not-rotating status. She maneuvered the craft so that we were able to see the planet out the porthole without rotation. Having achieved that, she then oriented the craft with the rocket end pointed to the eastern edge of the planet, precisely five miles above the surface. Then, she fired up the rocket and we started to decelerate, from our coasting speed of 45,000 miles per hour, at a rate of around 1000 miles per hour, per minute. After a 30-minute burn, using most of our remaining rocket fuel, we were down to orbit velocity on Mars, 15,000 mph, and in orbit at an elevation of roughly five miles above the surface. Sister Margie of course had practiced this on simulators many times during training. Sister Marsha and I also had done it a few times, so we were all capable to do it if for any reason Sister Marsha, unfortunately, was still in her own world, strapped tightly to her cot, and I was saddened by the thought that she would not experience the landing. She seemed at least able to feed and drink water for herself, and was occasionally awake. But she probably had no clue of what was going on. She had amnesia of some sort. Retrograde amnesia is when you cannot remember the past, prior to the trauma. Anterograde amnesia is when you are unable to remember things in short term or long term memory. Sister Margie seemed to have both. It was not clear, from what little I had to read, that she would recover completely, partially, or at all. Her brain may have suffered permanent damage. We had to continue on with the assumption that she was never going to be able to help us. I checked her straps, told her we are landing, and then I joined Marsha in the control section.

With Margie at the controls, we then orbited Mars confirming that our orbit was circular and our altitude was stable, varying slightly due to terrain. We continued our descent slowly as Margie applied rocket burns gradually, watching the gauges as she pulled on the fuel supply lever. After another ten minutes we were down to approximately 1000 feet elevation, and 1000 miles per hour, streaking across the sky on Mars. Margie set coordinates for our landing spot, near Nipigon Crater, into the computer, as we were trained. We needed to start our decent at a time which would bring us to land at the planned location. Margie used the rocket to gradually slow the craft as we began to feel atmospheric friction. The friction caused us to press back in our seats as we had our backs to the rear of the craft. At 500 mph, an alarm sounded, signaling that it was time to deploy the parachute. We strapped in tightly and prepared for the jolt of the chute.

The chute popped out and we felt the sudden jerk as the lines tightened and the craft slowed. Our velocity continued to drop, 400, 300, 200, 100 mph. At the same time we slowed to 100mph, our altitude dropped similarly, and read 100 feet above the surface. Under 100 mph the time had come to release the chute and fall the final distance under retro-rocket power. The remaining rocket fuel and oxygen was down to ten percent, easily adequate for landing. Sister Margie extended and fired up the landing rockets and switched to the auto-landing mode. The chute released, computers and gyros leveled us and we slowly descended, 80, 40, 20, 10 feet above the surface. As we descended, our foreward air speed reduced gradually, so that we were at speed zero at altitude 10 feet. the gradual setdown occurred without any problem, with barely perceptible sensation of having hit the surface. We could feel that the footpads sank into the sand completely and the craft lay flat on the desert floor like an egg, gently laying on a nest.

We were, to say the least, excited. I whooped. Sister Margie unstrapped and lept with joy, literally, hitting her head with a thud on the top of the craft. We laughed. Here we were on the surface of Mars! We looked out the portholes and saw sand and rocks. For the first time ever in the history of mankind, humans had travelled to another planet! It was a historic moment in the history of mankind. We were silent with awe. We high-fived; Margie and I congratulated ourselves. Marsha slept through it all.

Sister Margie checked the gauges. The outdoor temperature

measured 58 Fahrenheit in the mid-morning Sun. The pressure was low but as expected. The oxygen content outside was .3%. Then she checked our situation in the craft. Our temperature was 62 F. Due to our shortage and rationing program after the meteor hit back on infamous day 13, our pressure was really low, similar to that outdoors. Craft oxygen was similar to outdoors, .3%. As we travelled, we gradually, without pain or even notice, had reduced pressure and air to the point where it very nearly matched the atmosphere on Mars! "Maybe we don't need suits?" Margie claimed with a slight suggestion of surprise, or perhaps, sarcasm. We went silent, in a state of wonder, for a minute.

"Let's pop the door open!" I said, not thinking too deeply about the consequences. "Now wait a minute," Sister Margie countered, while checking the readings on the gauges. "We are sitting here, on a lifeless planet, with hardly enough air supply to last more than a few days, with barely enough water to get by for a week, almost no food, no chance in hell of going home, and in fact we're hungry as hell and emaciated, and you want to just pop the door open and walk out, as if we were on Earth? I think we need to discuss this a bit. I mean, what, exactly, are we going to do here?" I said, "Wait a minute. What, precisely, have we got left to lose? What if we crack the door open just a tad and then wait and see what happens? There is no pressure differential. The oxygen amount is nearly the same, inside and out. All we can see through the portal is sand. If something, anything at all happens, like we smell something, or feel funny at all, we'll seal the door."

She approached the lock, and turned the wheel, disengaging the multiple latches. The door backed off due to the compressed rubber gaskets. She pushed the door out just a bit. Nothing happened. We could see the sunlight glowing around the door edges. Then she stood back and waited. I stared at the door. After about a minute, Sister Margie said, "I don't smell anything." I added to that, "No pressure differential. It seems even fresher than the cabin air." (Which was pretty foul after two months journey.) Sister Margie then approached the door again and pushed it open a bit further, so there was a gap of several inches between the door and the craft. We could see the dim sunlight, but also, we could see light tan-colored sand and a pale light beige sky. We sat, stared, and waited another minute. Nothing happened. There was an eerie stillness and quiet until Sister Margie again approached the door and kicked it wide open. The door swung out and we saw a clear view of the desert sitting before us. We stood together in the doorway of the craft and stared out the door, glancing at each other momentarily, back and forth, with dropped jaws. "We're on Mars!" I exclaimed. "And we don't need air or suits!" Margie exclaimed, with a soft chuckle, as she lifted her hand and slapped herself on the forehead. We both looked at Sister Marsha in her bed, who missed it all.

Sister Margie, although she was next to the door, proposed that I should be the first to step out on the surface, because I was the oldest as well as the biggest and strongest, although we were both weak and atrophied. I crawled over to the doorway. I sat on the edge of the floor at the doorway, hanging my feet over the edge of the opening, and looked out. At the bottom of the door, there was light sand, about the same level as the floor of the craft. I was dressed in my jump suit with some tightly strapped boots and socks. I held on to the door jamb and placed a foot on the sand. The sand gave way! It was a lot like water, not sand. Ripples flowed in the sand around the spot where I set my foot ever deeper, as the sand seemed to move around, flowing over my foot. My foot went down until the sand was halfway to my knee, with no support. So I sat on the floor of the craft, for a minute, dangling both feet into the sand. There's got to be a bottom there somewhere, I thought. Slowly I put my right foot lower, and still, no bottom. As I got to the middle of my thigh, I decided to push off, much like easing into a swimming pool from its rim. I sank down, farther and farther, until I was chest deep in sand.

I sank into the sand and it flowed around me much like water on Earth. My body sank further, to my neck. Then I stopped sinking, as if I was floating. I looked down and felt with my gloved hand under the sand. Sister Margie asked, "Any thing to eat down there?" I reached down with my bare hand and felt something stringy, and yanked it up to the surface where I could see it. I recognized it immediately. Seaweed; green, soft, vegetable-like weeds. "Hey. Will this do? I asked. I pulled up bunches of it for a few minutes and before long, we had a pile of it, sitting on the floor of the craft, plenty for a meal for the three of us. It was with difficult credulity that I realized, there was water about three feet below the surface. We put a cloth down to absorb some of it, and wrung it out into a cup. I tasted it. Aside from a bit of sand, it was fresh, relatively clean, clear, odorless water!

We collected several pots full of water, using a cloth to absorb it, then wringing the cloth into a pot, then took the seaweed and washed it clean with the water. We put it in a pot and boiled it. The water boiled immediately, with hardly any fuel at all, at a very low temperature, about sixty degrees fahrenheit. We soon realized there was not much point to the boiling, as there was so little heat, how could it kill bacteria? Was there any bacteria? We both knew, there's only one way to find out. We were so hungry, we started eating it right out of the pot, raw seaweed, with our hands. We continued to do this, for an hour, cleaning, then eating, until our shrunken, shriveled stomachs were full of seaweed. And we were satisfied. I closed the door as the sun sank near the horizon, and the temperature dropped, so I turned on the fuel-cell-powered heater for our first experience of the frigid night of Mars. We crawled to our beds and slept, through the remaining few hours of sunlight, and well into the night. "Good night, Margie". "G'night Mark". "G'night, Marsha." We all slept deeply.

4

MEETING A MARTIAN

Sol 2 (February 20, 2027)

As sunshine broke through the porthole, Brother Mark arose from deep sleep, while Sister Marsha remained semi-conscious and Sister Margie continued sleeping soundly in the sleeping section. They had gone through an exhausting day during their landing the day before, and, having landed finally at their destination, and feeling constant gravity for the first time in months, they all slept long and hard without floating off the bed. For the first time in two months, they could abandon their necessary schedule from control room to play room and sleep room. The seaweed they ate for dinner the evening before was the first real sustenance, other than gluck, that they had eaten for months. It had been chewy, yet satisfying, as anything is good when you are emaciated and hungry. The meal strained their muscles on their jaws, as atrophy was evident throughout their bodies.

They were all scrawny now, nothing like the healthy astronauts that had trained on Earth just months prior. Their bones were protruding beneath their skin, and they resembled walking skeletons, like people in the concentration camps in the holocaust during WWII. Their muscles were sinewy and barely enough to move around the ship. Their faces, once full, colorful and puffy, now were like skulls with skin stretched over them. The low gravity on Mars, however, assisted their movements. On Earth, Brother Mark, previously a 120-pound, athletically fit,, small but well-proportioned, square-shouldered man, was down to about only thirty Mars-pounds, still able to hop around due to the low gravity of Mars. The Sisters, 100 pounds when they left Earth, were now much lighter. Marsha, having trouble eating regularly, due to her condition, and Margie, having to ration the precious gluck carefully at every meal, were each now down to only 20 Mars-pounds at most. Their clean-shaven, well-fed appearance on Earth gave them a bright and healthful appearance when they left, but now they were bolemic and bony like walking skeletons, and hairy, as Brother Mark had a two month beard and the women had untrimmed hair on their underarms and legs, with bushy-looking hair sticking out on their heads, six months growth, two or three inches long, almost globe-shaped, sticking out from their heads like spheres. They would be barely recognizable to their support team if only they could see them.

As the sunlight hit her face, Sister Marsha opened her eyes and saw that on the opposite side of the sleeping module, Brother Mark had already gotten out of his wall mounted sleeping cot. She turned on her stomach and leaned her head over the edge of her cot, and gazed over to the control module where she saw him open the exterior door. It was midmorning and the frigid -100 degree F night air had retreated, as the sun had risen and warmed the morning ground and air. The open door brought in a cool draft, and bright sunlight streamed into the control room as the sun rose ever higher.

Brother Mark, after opening the door to the craft, then sat down in front of the open door on the floor, legs dangling over the sill and feet dipping into the sand. The rising bright midmorning sun reflected on the surface of the sand. It was nearly as bright as on a hazy day on Earth, but noticeably smaller. He could not fix his eyes on the sun, as it was too bright, but he stared in its direction and inwardly felt gratitude that he had endured the voyage and now was able to appreciate the morning sunlight for still another day, or "sol", as they call it on the "Red Planet". They had gotten through a first night on Mars. The extreme cold had not been a problem, as the battery-powered heating elements kept it cozy inside the craft during the night. Mark then thought that he must bring out the solar panels to charge the batteries or they could freeze in a day or two. He breathed in deeply, allowing the thin, dry, cold air to penetrate his lungs. He felt he had to breathe more heavily than usual, deeper and more frequently, but he did not need supplemental oxygen. He stared through the circular doorway and studied the scene before him.

He gazed to the far hills. He wanted to see hills with green grass or trees, any kind of vegetation; but the hills were dry and rocky, and the sand was everywhere. Of course he knew that, and had seen pictures from the rovers of past during training, from Curiosity, Pathfinder, Viking, etc. He was prepared for the desolate, lifeless landscapes, and had committed to spending the rest of his life in that bleak, dry, environment, due mostly to the hypno training but also just due to his personal logical approach to everything. He knew he had no choice, but now, staring at reality in the face, as they say, "taking the tiger by the tail and looking the situation straight in the eye", he had to remind himself of his commitments and mission purpose, and said to himself out loud, although his voice was high-pitched, and the Sisters both overheard. "We are here." And he then noticed his voice was not as before, as if he inhaled air from a hydrogen balloon.

Adamus

Adamus was not a typical Arian (Martian) guy. But even the word "typical" as on Earth (Arth) has problems on Ares. Very different from most Martians, however many trillions or gazillions of them there may be, he was obsessed, from childhood, with "Blue Planet" Arth. In fact, he may be only one in a hundred or a thousand, on Mars, who even thought of Arth much at all. From a child, when his father first showed him Arth in a telescope which he gave him at the winter solstice of his fifth year, (ten Arth-years) he was fascinated with it. And then at age six, he spent a good deal of his early life just listening to his radio, a winter solstice gift from his father, and the sounds he could pick up, beaming from the sky kept his unmitigated attention. His fascination paid off well, as he gradually learned to set the frequency and focus on the sounds, and ultimately, over many years, understand and speak Arthtalk, (mostly English). He came to know it well enough that he could visualize in his mind what was happening on Arth. He had absorbed, through his the problems caused by the weather on Arth: hurricanes, quakes, tornadoes, wildfires and such calamities were regularly reported on the news. Likewise, over time, he learned about the horrors of Arth wars, as the reports of people killed and wounded by bombs and massacres, daily murders and thefts, came over the radio frequently, day and night. And the traffic jams, auto collisions, plane crashes, ships sinking... he heard about it all. It was so fascinating to him because there was so little on Mars like that. They had dust storms, but they were just occasional: quakes, sandstorms, meteors, and their effects, with people dying daily, were commonly occuring in his community and they dealt with them. He felt sorry for the people on Arth. They must suffer a lot, he thought. He felt a need to help them, and the more he listened, the more he hoped that some day he could go there.

On Adamus' seventh birthday, his father gave him a rara. It was a device that could simply play back sounds over and over. Adamus used this to record many of his radio listenings, and one in particular caught his attention firmly. It was the song, "A, B, C". He knew at first hearing that it was similar in both sound and melody to one he had learned as a child, "ah, be, da" and he used it to learn the alphabet on Arth by listening to it over and over. He studied the song, wrote down the letters, and compared to Ares letters. He came to realize the differences. Arthtalk has 26 letters, while Arestalk has only 20. But the two alphabets were strikingly similar. There is, as he learned, no C, P, Q, W, X, Y, or Z. He told his father about that and his father praised him for his good studies and explained: "Many beople, all over Mars, have different kultures, but they all have alfabets that are similar. So, as many others on Ares also have klaimed, Arth is nothing more than an ancient kolony of Martians who went there thousands of ars ago."

Being different, Adamus didn't socialize much with other kids. But he studied Arth dutifully, as if it was the most important thing in his life. Other kids didn't treat him well. Some bullied or teased him, others just ignored him. But most of that treatment simply caused him to spend more time with his radio, rara, and telescope. Then there was a girl in his neighborhood that he knew well; Ivana. One day he talked to her and explained many things about Arth to her, and she listened to him, the only other person, other than his father, who actually WAS interested. And she came to like him and learn Arthtalk with him. As they studied together one evening, while lying on a rock and watching the sunset, a fiery shooting star passed across the sky and over the horizon at the edge of nearby Nipigon crater. And Adamus knew what it was…the reverse slowdown burn of the exploratory craft from Arth, "MarsX". He had heard about it on the radio and was expecting it at the time of the opposition, as the Arth lined up with Mars and the Sun. And today, he knew, Arth was in line with the setting Sun. But he did not know where it would come down. He hoped it would come down near him.

Moving Rocks

As Brother Mark stared out the open circular hatch, he gazed to the far hills. He thought about his mission, and what he had to do. They were all hungry, there was nothing left of their food, but they had plenty of water, all around them, as he discovered the day before. He had to find food for himself and the two sisters. "What are we going to do, eat seaweed until we die?" he thought to himself, and expelled a sigh of helplessness, slowly moving his head from side to side.

He saw the sand, outside the door, rippling like water. "Maybe there are fish under the sand?" He pondered the seaweed they found under the sand. Things, he realized now, are not as desolate as they had been led to believe, on Mars.

He saw the rocks, sitting on the sand. There was something strange about them. He didn't believe it at first, and so he wiped his eyes, as if maybe something was causing the strange sight he had before him. They were moving! He closed his eyes and then opened them wide, still in disbelief. The rocks were moving! The sand rippled like water, and the rocks moved! It was completely unlike the stolid, bleached out still photos he had studied from Mars rovers, during training.

Sister Margie saw him wipe his eyes, and deduced that he had seen something strange. She asked, "Brother Mark, what is it?" He said, "The rocks are moving." He said it softly, in high-pitched voice, with a bit of wonder and a bit of confusion, while he continued to stare out the doorway. Sister Margie got out of her sleeping cot and crawled over to his side and stared at the sight before them. What looked like rocks were clearly moving. Not just one, but several. They seemed to be circling the craft, but at a distance.

Meeting Adamus

After seeing the reverse burn the night before with Ivana, Adamus, unable to sleep, arose early before dawn and went around his neighborhood and tried to learn anything he could about the location of the landing. On Ares, there are no radio stations broadcasting the news. News is obtained through word of mouth. And people talk a lot, (like gossip), especially regarding skywatchers' observances such as meteors, comets, and spaceships from outside Ares. There had been several noted spacecraft landings in the past, so people knew how to differentiate them from meteors; the latest was in a crater halfway around the planet, six years earlier. It had turned out to be an unmanned exploratory device, from Arth.

Adamus learned that the craft, which came down just a few hours before sundown the day before, had landed near Nipigon crater. It was not just one report; everyone in the community that he came across was talking about it. People were excited to the hilt. There was something that landed just yesterday, in THEIR vicinity! This was definitely something to talk about. But people did not know anything else. They did not know, as Adamus knew, that it was from Arth, and that it was the first <u>manned</u> spacecraft from Arth to Ares, called "MarsX". Adamus knew this was an opportunity for him, and him alone, to use his Arthtalk abiity, and prepared to head for the center of the crater. He lived near the center of the crater, a matter of a good walk. It was a fairly long journey, considering the difficulty of the sands, and he needed to prepare for several hours, perhaps the entire day. He took some food and water, for both himself and his mount, and climbed upon a gorth which had been roaming his neighborhood of late.

A gorth is an animal, a reptile, which looks like a rock but has large padded feet, good for travelling in the terrain of Ares. The bumps on its back make it easy to mount. And with a nice prod, a long stick, the animal can be directed in a desired direction. It is entirely safe, as the animal is a vegetarian beast, with enough brains (like dogs, cats, and horses, to know that if it follows the proper direction it will be well rewarded with food and water, and enough smarts to respect humankind as leaders. Training a gorth is a lot like training a dog or any other animal. You gain its faith and you reward it with food, and it obeys your commands. And his gorth was well trained.

After explaining his intentions to Ivana, Adamus set off towards the center of the crater on the gorth.

A few hours after sunrise he saw, through his telescope, the glint of the golden cylindrical craft, lying on the sand, in the far distance. He prodded his gorth and continued on his way. Soon he was close enough to see the craft easily. As he approached the craft he headed his gorth straight towards the large circular doorway.

Two of the scrawny, hairy, old Earthly occupants of the golden cylinder sat in the doorway on the floor of the craft, too weak to stand but in awe, staring with disbelief at the rocks that moved about them. Margie continued to lie on her cot in the sleeping section, awake but unawarestaring at the wall. Brother Mark noticed that the "rocks" seemed to keep their distance, perhaps a rock-throw away in distance. One of the "rocks", however, was headed straight towards them, and was slowly getting closer.

Adamus guided his gorth alongside the open doorway, lifted his right arm with palm open, as the ancient gesture of peace, and simply yelled firmly, cupping his hands for a megaphone effect, "Hello. I am Adamus. Welkome to Mars."

Adamus on Gorth   (Curiosity Photo)

Staring at the moving rock and the small figure mounted upon it, astonished, Brother Mark lifted his right arm and open palm, and returned the greeting. "Hello, Adamus, I am Brother Mark, and with me are Sisters Margie and Marsha, (he gestured inside the craft). We come from planet Earth." Sister Margie held up her right hand in the ancient universal peace gesture, best known as the way for American immigrants to greet American indigenous peoples. The two astronauts and the Martian traded glances, not knowing what to do or say, just taking in what had just happened and living the surprise.

Sustenance

Adamus explained in his best Earthtalk that he was anxious to help them in any way they needed. "I will be glad to help you."Brother Mark then explained their dire situation: no food, starving, weak, and not knowing where to find food or water, and in fact, not knowing what to expect. Adamus asked, "What kind of food do you want?" Brother Mark explained that they were all three astronauts vegetarians, but were willing to eat most anything as they are so starved, malnourished and weak from the journey. Adamus then reached down to his knapsack and lifted it so that Brother Mark could reach out and take it. Brother Mark took the tiny little bag, (about the size of a small cloth purse), grasping it between his thumb and forefinger, and said "What's this?" "Inside you find three kakes." These were for my gorth, but I think he can wait a bit. You go ahead and eat those." Brother Mark opened the bag and poured the three wafers into his palm. They were the size and shape of dimes, white like wafers. He gave one to Sister Margie, and another he hopped over and put in Sister Marsha's mouth. They each put them in their mouths and chewed, voraciously. The sweet flavor, soft texture, and light brown color reminded them of banana nut bread. They swallowed and Sister Margie remarked, "How delicious!" Sister Marsha nodded in agreement. Brother Mark said to Adamus, "That is wonderful. But we need a lot more. As you can see, we are big people compared to you. Can you bring us more?"

Adamus asked, trying not to sound too businesslike, as most Martians did with near instinctiveness, "Do you have anything to um, compensate for my troubles?" "Um, I don't know", said Mark. "We have eaten everything in our craft. There's nothing much left. There might be something in the cargo bay, but it will take me some time to check. We haven't opened it since we landed." "Fine," said Adamus, "I'll go get you more food and be back soon."

With that, Adamus departed, slowly scooting away on his gorth towards a group of similar moving rocks in the distance. Brother Mark decided to open the cargo bay. He got a phillips screwdriver from the control room toolbox and sank down into the sand and "swam" over to the cargo bay. Up to his chest in sand, he unscrewed the panel and looked inside. He could see the tanks for gluck, water, and air, and their tubing that conveyed them to the craft. He could see that an ice meteor had ruptured several of the lines. In a corner of the bay, he found a rectangular tin box, actually a "Superman" lunch box. The box appeared to have been dented by the ice meteor, and in fact, appeared to have protected some of the tubing for the gluck, water, and air. On the top was a postit, inscribed "Best of luck, from Louis". He pried open the box and found inside four canisters, all undamaged by the meteor, which were labeled "coffee", "tea", "salt', and "pepper". And, to top it off, the care package included a pint of peach brandy.

A similar box, a "Wonder Woman" lunch box, was labeled "SEEDS". Brother Mark knew what that was, as they had gone through a training session about it. Inside were dozens of different packages of seeds. They were to plant them all in a garden after arriving and establishing a garden site, building a greenhouse, and finding a source of water.

He tapped his screwdriver on the tanks. Each one made a sound like "bong" and sounded empty. Truly, they had nothing but seeds and the wonderful gifts from Louis.

The Feast

Adamus returned on his gorth. He had gone around to ask other Martians on nearby gorths for cakes and cans of water. Everyone carried some for thrir gorths and were glad to give them to the poor, staarving Earthling astronauts. Altogether, he managed to find three dozen cakes and a dozen tiny water cans, each can about the size of an appothecary pill. He asked Brother Mark to get some bowls and cups to put the cakes and water into them. Brother Mark complied, and the men put a dozen cakes into each bowl and poured four canteens of water into each small cup. Brother Mark then set them in front of Sister Marsha beside him, and took one bowl and one cup to Margie and they began to eat and drink the tiny morsels. Margie remained in her cot, unable to join them. Marsha would give the small portion of sustenance to Margie later.

After swallowing his first little cake, and drinking a sip of water, Brother Mark turned to Adamus and told him, "I think I may have found something in the cargo bay that you might like." The Sisters, likewise, stopped eating and watched Brother Mark. He opened the tin gift box from Louis and brought out the metal canisters, many seeds and spices, salt and pepper, setting them on the floor of the craft. He opened them and took a small pinch of each, one by one, and put on the floor in front of the men.

Adamus looked at them and then, after a few minutes, then

turned to Brother Mark and said "Brother Mark, these are some of the most brecious things on Ares. If you give me but half of those kontainers, it will be sufficient to employ me as your helper for many months." With that, Brother Mark and Sister Marsha continued to eat their cakes and sip their bowls of water…their first real meal in two months, allbeit miniscule. They passed around the peach brandy from Louis, and each took a swig from it with each pass. Adamus asked about the drink. Brother Mark then took a small spoon and poured a swig of brandy. Adamus sat near the spoon and leaned over the edge to take a drink using his cupped hands, and then another and another, until, after a few moments, he was laughing and swaggering around, quite inebriated. Adamus then told the astronauts, "I must return to my home now. I'll try to bring you much more food and water. I'll be back soon." The astronauts smiled at each other as . They stumbled away and waved as the gorth turned and slipped away in the sand. The two asyronauts, likewise a bit inebriated from Louis' gift, smiled and laughed for the first time in their recent memories. They consumed the cakes and water and half of the brandy, and in a few moments, the bowls were empty, and the astronauts lay down on the floor of the craft to absorb the nutritients. And tgey began to heal.

Adamus Returns

After a short time, Adamus returned, with plenty of food and drink. As the men with him unloaded their goods to the floor of the craft just inside the doorway, Adamus stood up on his mount and yelled through a megaphone.

"Honestly," Adamus shouted up at the astronauts, "I am kuite disappointed in what I am seeing in u. Here we on Mars have come to expect that when the Arthmen finally kame, they would be in full and kolorful astronaut suits and helmets, ioung and healthful, good examples of your peoples. But looking at you now, I see an old man and two old iomen, dressed in their undies, with skraggly hair all over, and smelly and skrawny like people who have been kiked out of their homes. It's a bit strange and disappointing, I'm sorry to say. I hope I don't offend you."

Brother Mark offered, with understandable embarrassment, "Of course, we have been through a horrible ordeal, traveling from our planet to yours. We are barely alive, due to a storm of ice meteors that nearly destroyed our ship and killed us all. Our food and water, as well as our air supply, are nearly gone. We are grateful to be alive. You can tell us anything and we will be glad to hear it. Perhaps we should talk, seriously? Let's get to a place where you don't have to shout through a megaohone and we have to strain to hear you. Let me lift you up and take you to our table, and I'll sit in a chair beside you, and we will discuss many important things."

"Fine, iuonderful, eksellent," replied Adamus. He was entirely thrilled with the way things were going. He seemingly had gotten on a good footing with his newfound Arth friends. He briefly thought back at how he learned and became fluent in Arthtalk by studying radio transmissions, and came to be what he was now, an interplanetary communicator and translator. He could barely contain his happiness. His lifelong dreams were coming true.

At The Table

Adamus climbed into Brother Mark's upfaced palm, and Mark carefully picked him up and carried him into the craft to the table, where he placed him gently thereupon. Marsha had pulled down the table, hinged off of the wall. Mark took a paper napkin and placed it in the center of the round table, like a pad, for Adamus to sit on like a blanket. He and the sisters then sat down on the floor at the table, which was like a coffee table, just a foot in height above the floor, and about three feet in diameter. It was a steel disk that had protractible legs and hinges that held it securely to the wall or floor, but it could be removed around wherever it was appropriate, if necesssary. During the voyage it had been placed on the "floor" of the r&r room, which, due to tumble, was a place of gravity, but now, was on a wall in the control room.

Brother Mark asked, "Would you like something to drink while we talk?" We have a bit of the brandy left. I'm afraid there isn't much else…just some water we gathered outside the craft. We filtered it and put it in containers so it wouldn't evaporate.

"Please, " replied Adamus, "I would love to have more of that delicious drink?"

And so began the discussion of a lifetime, the first discussion between Earthlings and a Martian.

First Talk

Sol 2 (February 20, 2027)

Brother Mark then took a microphone from the wall and placed it on the table next to Adamus. As Adamus spoke, without yelling, his words were amplified magnificently to a level that could be easily heard by the astronauts.

Brother Mark then took the brandy bottle, now half full, and poured a drop of it onto the table next to Adamus, who dipped his tiny finger into it and stuck it into his mouth, with great pleasure. "Really good," he exclaimed.

The three of them went on to nibble on the dime-sized wafers that Adamus had brought them, and the brandy that Louis Newcastle had secretly stowed, and Adamus and Sister Marsha and Brother Mark each sipped from a small teacup of brandy in front of them. Sister Margie lay in her cot, able to hear, but still with no clue about where she was or what was happening. As they sipped and consumed the tiny but chewey wafers, the discussion began.

Brother Mark said, "If you were the same size as me, you would do well on Earth".

Adamus responded, "Are there beople my size on Earth?"

They sat silently for an awkward moment, trying to start the incredibly momentous conversation, but wondering where to start or what to say or how to say it. It was an event like the first meeting of Columbus with natives of the New Continent...extremely significant, yet at least language was not a barrier.

Brother Mark finally answered: "No, there are no people as small as you; in fact, we are small compared to most of the people on Earth. Ok let's take turns. I'll ask a question, then you ask me one."

"Okay, your turn," replied Adamus.

And so Mark asked, "How is it that you are able to speak almost perfect English?"

Adamus replied, "I'm self taught. I listened to the radio ever since my father gave it to me when I was a small shild, for many years. I am brobably the only one on Mars that kan speak your language. I know all about your blanet, Arth. I studied your alphabet and recorded sentences, then listened karefully and studied the words. Your language is similar to ours. Your alphabet is similar to ours. Our elders tell us we are related, from long, long ago. Now my turn. Why did u kome to Mars?"

Brother Mark pauses a few seconds, then began. "Our mission is to come to Mars, to live and to explore. We need to look for things that will help Earthlings in the future to travel here and make it financially useful and practical to come in the future. We need to look for minerals like gold or silver, which are prescious and rare on Earth. We are also hoping to find artifacts of olden times. We have seen phoyographs of Mars that suggest there are many things here from Earth. We are also looking for different animals, plants, and people, and fossils or gemsyones, anything that we may be able to return to Earth some day. We are looking for materials for survival such as food and water. We come from the country called America. It is the best country on Earth. It is called the "land of the free". It is a country that everyone wants to go to from all over Earth. Do you have a mission. Adamus? And do you have a country?"

And Adamus replied. "Yes, I have a mission. My mission is to some day go to Earth. But also I have heard of this land of the free that is Amerika. I hope that some day, somehow, I will be able to travel to Earth and live in the "land of the free", Amerika. I have had this wish for most of my life, since I first heard of it. No, we do not have countries on Mars. We are all one country. It is a country that is ruled by a military establishment. We must do as we are told. It is not free, like Amerika. So let me ask you now, will you take me there when you return?"

"I'm sorry" said Brother Mark. "We can not not return. Our craft is not designed to return to Earth. We were barely able to survive the voyage to Mars, but also, it was part of our mission to "live and die on Mars". We have some extra rocket fuel left over, about ten percent, but that is not much, certainly not enough for us to return."

Adamus then asked: "I am just a very small person compared to you so it would take a lot less energy and a smaller, lighter spaceship. Also to go to Earth is "downhill" relative to Sun's gravity, so it is like "falling". And also to get off of Mars takes less energy than to get off of Earth, because it is smaller. It might be possible to use some of your leftover rocket fuel to get me to Earth. What do you think?"

Brother Mark: "I will consider it but for now I just don't know. Marsha? What do you think?"

Marsha said, "I think we might be able to detach the nose cone, parachute and supply bay and reattach it to the rocket engine and fuel bay. It seems feasible. That means we would keep the living portions here on Mars for ourselves. We don't have any supplies like food and water left anyway. If only Margie were conscious, she would be able to go through the calcs to see if it would work with the fuel available. I just don't know about that."

Brother Mark: "Maybe we could send back some artifacts or gold coins. Tell us Adamus, how can we get out and search for that sort of thing?

Adamus: "We need to get you off of this sand-filled swamp first, to dry land. We are not going to find any gold coins or artifacts in this sand-covered swamp. We need to get to higher and dryer land, where things are not sinking into the sand. Tomorrow we could make an exkursion. I need to get home soon today to gather more food for you tomorrow morning and to arrange for some kind of transportation, a big gorth for each of you, yo get to solid ground, for our ekskursion. Then we can walk by foot to the edge of the crater nearby; I could ride on your shoulder while you walk. It's not far."

Brother Mark turned to Sister Marsha who nodded in agreement and said: "We can eat seaweed for the time being. I would love to get out of this craft for awhile. Sister Margie will be okay without us, I'm quite sure."

Adamus: "What's wrong with her? She seems really sick."

Brother Mark: " She had an iron meteor shoot through the wall of our craft and into her head. I managed to remove it with magnets but she still seems to have amnesia and has just been sort of withdrawn and unable to talk or move or anything for over a month. She just lies on her cot and we feed her and she drinks but otherwise seems healthy. I'm afraid she can't be of much use to us. She doesn't seem to realize that we are on Mars, or why."

Adamus: "I know very little about medisine. My girlfriend is studiing to be a nurse. I'll ask her if she kan do anithing. In fact I might bring her with us on the exkursion. She kould look at Sister Margie in the morning and bossibly help her. But now the Sol is koming klose to the point when I must go home. I must be home before Solset. The kold at night must be avoided. It kan freeze people kompleteli like roks."

Brother Mark: "So where do you live?"

Adamus: "I live underground, not far from here. I can get home on my gorth in an hour."

And so Brother Mark put down his uupfaced palm for Adamus to step into it and Adamus was taken to the entryway of the craft, where he called his gorth with hand claps. The gorth came and took him home.

Adamus was very proud of the progress he had made during the day. He went home, told his parents a bit about it, and then went to his neighbor Ivanka and others, to arrange food and gorths for the following sol.

5

EXCURSION ON MARS

PREPARATION

Sol 2 (February 20, 2027) Late afternoon

The astronauts were content to gather more seaweed from the underground lake, and to gather water, as well, as they had from the day before. They gathered enough for several days worth of meals. They found several types of seaweed and sorted it out. They found large fish and eels living in the water beneath their craft, but being vetetarian, they chose to be satisfied with the seaweed. Sister Marsha studied the nutrition of kelp on the computer while Brother Mark gathered the kelp and water.

Sister Marsha found that Kelp is actually a staple in Japanese and Korean food. It is very nutritional and has most of the vitamins and minerals needed for healthy living. The only problem is that it is lacking in the B vitamin family, and it is relatively low in calories so one must consume large quantities to sustain. What is needed is some kind of grain to supplement it, such as rice, which is good in B vitamins and also high in calories. Again, that is a staple in Asian countries. She found that Kelp can be dried in the sun and stored for later use.

Sister Margie, being of Japanese ancestry, would probably have known about that if she were conscious and able to help the other two astronauts.

The implication from her nutrition study was that they need rice, or some kind of grain. The ability to grow rice on Mars did not seem very possible, considering the cold nights. Rice is grown in more temperate climates on Earth, closer to the equator. However, Sister Marsha found through research that rice is grown in Alaska, so it might conceivably grow in lower temperatures with some kind of greenhouse. Mars is farther from the Sun than Earth, but the location of the landing site was unfortuately at a relatively high latitude, (36 degrees) and so the sunlight at that location does not seem very amenable to growing rice. They decided to ask Adamus in the morning when he returned, if he knows anywhere on Mars where rice or other grains can be grown. Also, what was that waferlike food that he called "gorth food"? It seemed like some kind of bread. Maybe they could get enough to rely on for their food source.

Brother Mark harvested what seemed to be an endless amount of the kelp, enough for several days; he rinsed it, and dried it by hanging it on a rack in front of the solar-powered heater in the craft. They simply needed to soak it in water before eating. Also he gathered up a lot of water which they filtered and put in containers. They ate and drank until satisfied, fed some to Margie, and so ended their second sol.

Meanwhile, Adamus returned to his home and began to make arrangements for the following day. He went around to neighbors and arranged to pick up lots of gorth food in the morning, and he arranged for two large gorths for the two astronauts. He then met with Ivanka.

Ivanka listened to Adamus with deep interest in his story of a meeting with the Earthlings. It was totally fascinating to her. She wanted to help, particularly regarding the astronaut in a coma, or semi-conscious. She began to develop some ideas about what to do in the following day. She went to talk with a nearby doctor who happened to be knowledgale about neurology.

The doctor recommended that she check the wound carefully. If there was a sign of infection, there was a possibility that the problem could be caused by a cyst inside the brain, putting pressure on the part of the brain that regulates motivation. If that was not the case, then Ivanka probably could do little for the patient, who might remain in comatose state until eventually she died. She should be given plenty of food and water. Gorth food would probably be sufficient, as it contains lots of essential ingredients. If there was a cyst, it needed to be drained immediately, using a sharp instrument such as a straight pin or needle. Also, feed the patient coffee or tea. The caffeine may help to arrouse. She needed to check the patient for any kind of movement, such as fingers or eyelids. They might be used for communication purposes and to determine if she was mentally awake or totally unconscious.

Sol 3 (February 21, 2027)

The astronauts slept late to sit out the cold morning. They breakfasted on the kelp they had harvested the prior day.

Adamus and Ivanka met early in the morning to discuss the day ahead. Ivanka told Adamus about the doctor's recommendations. Adamus informed Ivanka about the arrangements for gorths and food for the astronauts. Adamus' parents helped to put the food into large cardboard boxes, "large" being a matter of personal opinion. Adamus waited for the cold night air to warm from the Sol for an hour or so. Then the two gathered the food and picked up the gorths from a nearby shelter, a sort of quanset building coverered with sand. They headed for the astronauts' craft, the two of them on one small gorth and two large gorths, one for each of the astronauts.

Gorths act a lot like horses on Earth. When trained well, they will do pretty much what they are desired to do as long as they are rewarded with food and water by their human drivers. They look like rocks but they have eyes and mouth and nostrils, and they have feet that are very wide and are able to walk on loose sand well without sinking into it. They can carry large numbers of minipeople or single people if large like the astronauts.

Adamus and Ivanka arrived wit the gorths at the craft door, and waited outside until Brother Mark opened the door. Brother Mark then reached out his hand and the two Martians then climbed into it and he took them into the craft yo the table where he had set up a microphone for Adamus the day before.

Adamus introduced Ivanka, saying she was his very nice friend and neighbor, and she was training to be a nurse. Ivanka then spoke in Marstalk to Adamaus, who translated to Earthtalk, talking into the microphone, saying Ivanka was very happy to meet Earthlings and also quite impressed with the astronauts' craft, the microphone and speaker setup, and the video monitors and craft control panels. She explained that she had met with a doctor the day before and discussed the situation of the unconscious astronaut, Sister Margie. She told the astronauts how she needed to check the wound for infection inside the skull and also that if there is a cyst it needed to be drained immediately, and that also she needed to check Sister Margie for signs of movement such as fingers and eyelid blinking. And also the patient may benefit from coffee and food. She would stay with the unconscious astronaut while Adamus and the other two went on their excursion.

Brother Mark expressed his heartfelt gratitude for Ivanka's concern for Sister Margie, and her coming to meet Earthlings. He explained that Sister Margie was a very important member of the crew, she was the one most experienced in technical calculations and simulations. In fact she had programmed the landing on Mars and the entire voyage, and she is needed to be returned to normal, if possible, to assist in their mission to explore Mars.

He went on to explain that the picture from old Earth rover photos, (on the monitor), showed many things that may at first glance look like rocks, but with close examination may be things that could be very valuable on Earth.

PIA00563 Viking 1 First Color Image   (Artifacts)

These were the types of things that he hoped to look for and find during the upcoming excursion, pointing to some of the possinle ancient artifacts from Earth that had been photographed by a rover sent to Mars many years in the past. (Viking 1, 1996, first photo)

Adamus then explained how he had arranged for three bags of gorth food, one for the patient, and one for each astronaut. The three bags were on the gorths waiting outside the craft door. He recommended that they leave promptly, and return mid-afternooon, after a short time, so that they don't get caught in the frigid evening air. Everyone agreed, and Adamus was placed on the small gorth while Brother Mark and Sister Marsha mounted the two large gorths, very similar to the way one would mount horses. Ivanka stayed behind, and had been placed on a table with a microphone, next to Sister Margie's cot next to her head wound, with a straight pin and small paper towels and a small container of rubbing alcohol, along with the bag of gorth food and water and some dried (dehydrated) coffee, diven to her by the doctor the night before. She would examine the wound, feed, and administer water with a straw. The gorths were mounted and the excursion then began.

It was still morning, well before noon. The excursion would last until mid-afternoon. The astronauts had eaten breakfast, just kelp. It was not completely satisfying but it was a good replacement for gluck, which they had lived on for the past two months. Adamus explained that to guide the gorths, they needed to simply lean in the direction they wanted to go. Also straight up was stop. So Lean foreward, go foreward, lean left, turn left, etc.

Adamus led them towards the hills in the distance. The hills were the edge of Nigipon Crater. The gorths were slow-moving but much better than trying to wade through the sand-covered lake. Beneath them were huge fish, sharks, eels, snakes, many things that were dangerous. After awhile they reached the end of the sand and they reached solid ground. Adamus drove his gorth next to Brother Mark's gorth and yelled to him to lift him to his shoulder. Brother Mark put him on his shoulder and then could hear him well as he shouted into his ear. Adamus clinged to Brother Mark's collar as Brother Mark dismounted, as did Sister Marsha.

"We can walk from here to the top of the hill," explained Adamus. "Just leave the gorths here. Oh, we should give them some pieces of food now and they will wait for us here. We need to go over the hill into the crater. Don't worry, nobody will bother us. Nobody goes into the crater. It is like a cemetery, full of dead people. Most people just stay away; it's a dead- man's land. We put our dead people in the crater, but otherwise, it is just a place to stay away from. I have never gone there before, myself."

Brother Mark, with Adamus on his shoulder, and alongside Sister Marsha, continued hiking on the solid ground, up to the top of the hill, which was the edge of the crater. From the top of the hill they could look down and see what looked like a vast sand-filled lake similar to where their craft had landed. There were rocks in the sand, and Adamus explained "Those are not rocks, they are heads of people who died. They just sort of float in the sand, and they decompose after a long time, over centuries. That one, the one that looks like a skull, it is thousands of years old. But that one, looking almost alive, (pointing), is just a few years old. We need to look along the crater edge for artifacts. The crater edge helped to capture debris from the Great Flood."

Sister Marsha was the first to notice an object, and exclaimed, "Look, there is a statue!" They worked their way down to the statue and examined it carefully. Brother Mark looked at his feet and saw many objects, man-made carved stone pieces and metal objects. In a few minutes they had gathered a handful of coins and metal objects, some gold, some silver, some bronze. They continued for awhile, putting their findings into a bag.

After a while, they had filled the bag, and Adamus told them "We had better go back to the craft now. We can come later and gather more, but we must head back because the Sol is getting to the point where we must leave." They headed back to the gorths, fed them and ate some of the gorth food themselves, and drank water from canteens. They mounted the gorths and headed west, where their craft, they could barely see, had landed.

MEANWHILE, BACK AT THE CRAFT

Ivanka had examined Sister Margie's wound. Pressing it with her palms, wiping it with alcohol, she pierced it with the straight pin, which was like a sword for her, then wiped it with a paper towel dipped in alcohol. She could tell it was abcessed, swollen. When she punctured the wound with the straight pin, blood mixed with white liquid flowed out which she absorbed with paper towels, many times. She pushed the wound with her hands and liquid continued to flow for awhile. She kept wiping it for a long time with paper towels and alcohol, until eventually it stopped oozing. Then she began to put dried coffee powder onto Sister Margie's lips. The patient consumed the dried coffee, like a subconscious reflex action of the lips and tongue. Ivanka watched the patient's hand and fingers, looking for movement; also she looked at the eyelids, hoping for any kind of blinking.

Astoundedly, in a short time, Sister Margie opened her eyelids widely and stared upward. She was awake! Ivanka ran across the table to the microphone and began to speak Marstalk, then realising that she was not understood, she said the one word she knew, in Earthtalk, "Hello!" She repeated it several times, and Sister Margie began to look around, finally settling and fucusing her eyes on the tiny human Martian woman. "Well hello!" she said.

Communicating in another language is difficult and frustrating, but they both realized the common problem right away. They both began using hand signals and gestures to try to make sense to each other. The tiny Martian woman pointed to herself and said loudly over the microphone, "Ivanka". The patient pointed to herself and said, "Sister Margie". She then asked, "Sister Marsha and Brother Mark?" raising her voice as in a question, gesturing with upfaced hands. Ivanka knew what she meant, and pointed to the hills outside the porthole. Sister Margie looked out the porthole and understood, looking at the vast dry sand, and realized instantly that she was now on Mars. She knew nothing about what she had gone through for the past many days, but she did realize that she had completed her journey, and was on Mars.

She attempted to sit on her cot but discovered that she was strapped down. She managed to unbuckle the straps and pushed herself to sitting position on the cot. She scooted the table over with her hand. She felt very weak but she knew that she needed to stand, and she tried. She first fell to her knees on the floor, then slowly stood up, shaking, again on her feet. Ivanka watched and smiled heartedly. Sister Margie then took a step...and another. Ivanka clapped in applause into the microphone, with "ooo's and aahs". Sister Margie laughed and breathed deeply. The two fist bumped, in what must be a universal sign of commoradarie.

Soon after that, the craft door opened. Brother Mark, Sister Marsha, and Adamus had returned from their excursion. The two stood in the doorway, and stared in awe at what they saw: Sister Margie standing up on her cot and Ivanka on the table next to her, both smiling and laughing. It took them awhile to grasp the incredible sight.

Sister Margie was quite happy to hear about the situation about the landing, the kelp, the Martians, the gorths and gorth food, and her cure from unconsciousness. She just listened to the others intently and responded weakly but intelligently. After joyous celebrations, Adamus and Ivanka left for home and the astronauts dined together on the meager food they had available, and finished off the brandy from Louis, then retired as the sun set. They excitedly explained to Sister Margie about she had been hit by a meteor, went unconscious and eventually was revived by Ivanka, how the landing went exactly as planned, how they found kelp right outside the craft door under the sand, how there was an underground lake under the ship, how they met Adamus, who brought them food, and how they had gone on an excursion to the edge of Nipigon Crater and found a bag full ancient artifacts. They all pored over the artifacts, several gold, silver, and copper coins and various other metal objects, like ancient tools and pottery, also bones and teeth of animals, which were arranged neatly on a table. But weak and malnourished, their excitement gradually succumbed to sleepiness, and after some time, they were all quite tired and needed rest, and retired to their cots. They all slept deeply.

6

COMMUNICATING WITH CONTROL

Sol 4 (February 22, 2027)

The three astronauts were awakened at dawn when they felt a sort of vibration of the craft. They first considered it an earthquake or meteor hit, and looked out the portholes for any evidence of change. Lo and behold, outside the door side of the craft, about fifty feet away from the door, appeared a vertically cylindrical craft, half-buried in the sand, smaller than their own, painted white, and with a large parachute that conveniently covered the sand between their craft and itself, and the craft had a logo upon it that read "MarsX", which stared at them remarkably and undoubtedly. It was understandably a craft sent by Louis Newcastle, likely with great importance, with something for their benefit. Perhaps food and water or some other supplies. It had to have been sent soon after they left, in fact, most likely after communications were lost on day 13 of the voyage.

Brother Mark opened the door, slipped down into the sand, and using the parachute as a walking surface, sank into the sand to his waist, and plodded through the sand to reach the second craft. He had brought a few tools, and as he got close, he saw that there was a removable panel. On the face of the panel was written "MarsX/ Control Communicator". He yelled to the Sisters, (in squeaky voice due to the low atmospheric pressure), "It's the spare communication panel from Louis."He removed the screws and pulled off the cover. Inside was a communication device similar to the damaged one that was in the craft control panel. At the side of the panel he could see miscellaneous goodies like bottles of liquer, purified water, snacks like potato chips, olives, pickles, and candy bars. He yelled to the Sisters, "Food and water!"

He studied the panel for awhile and flipped the toggle switch which turned on the battery powered communicator. He pushed down on the microphone button and spoke into it. "MarsX to Control, come in." He repeated it three times, and then he realized that there was a delay due to the long distance between the transmitter and receiver. There was a 70 million mile distance between Earth and Mars, and even at the speed of light, it takes awhile for the radio waves to reach Earth. Brother Mark yelled to Sister Margie, in part to test her abilities, and in part because he did not yet himself calculate the time involved; "How long does it take to transmit to Earth?" Sister Margie replied a few seconds later, "About two thirds of the time for light to reach Earth from the Sun, which is about six minutes." So Brother Mark realized that Sister Margie was back, and the three astronauts prepared for a twelve-minute wait. Brother Mark waded through the sand back to the craft and handed some of the goodies to the Sisters and they all gobbled up some of them and drank purified water from Earth. They were all famished.

Louis Newcastle, by himself, had anticipated the call from Mars and had excitedly stayed in the Control headquarters building next to the communicator. He had been able to see, through Mars satellite imagery, that the secondary communication gear had landed precisely where and when it had been planned, simply by viewing photos from an orbiting satellite. He was all alone. The rest of his staff of technicians had been released a month earlier, as the MarsX project was put on hold soon after loss of communications at the time of the meteor storm on Day 13. World situation had developed to help that decision. The communications gear was launched from Earth just two weeks later, and with that launch, there was little for anyone to do but wait, so Louis released the entire MarsX Conyrol team.

Upon hearing Brother Mark's squeaky voice, which he could barely recognize, Louis was thrilled, and replied immediately, "Brother Mark, is that you? Louis Newcastle at Control, to MarsX, over." And then he realized he had to wait for 12 minutes for each transmission. He waited, anxiously.

12 minutes later, Brother Mark replied: "We're all here on Mars. We adapted to the low oxygen and air pressure during the flight. We are exhausted and starving due to the flight but we have found some minimal sources of food and water. Thank you for the goodies. We have already consumed half of them. MarsX over."

HUMANITY IS ON THE BRINK

Louis then explained: "Earth is not well. We are hit with another virus, a variant of the Covid-19 virus. This one is killing everyone. I am lucky to be alive. Whole towns have died all over the country and around the world. People are falling like flies. It's just like the situation described in a novel published in 1969, and made into a movie which went public in 1971. so we call it the "Andromeda variant of Covid19". There seems to be no cure. The virus has overcome human immunity, vaccines, masks, everything we know. Humanity is on the brink. You three are lucky to have escaped. Louis, over."

During the six minute break, Brother Mark told the Sisters about it. They were shocked. But something was wrong with Brother Mark. he remembered having lost a daughter to a virus but very little else about his past. Brother Mark and the Sisters agreed that he should ask Louis about their past lives. They, similar to Brother Mark, remembered well their training but very little before that.Why was that? Maybe Louis knows something?

As the six minutes passed, Brother Mark again waded over to the communication gear and asked Louis:

"The world as we knew it is ending? Are you certain? We have a concern here that has built up ever since we lost communications on Day 13. We don't remember our pasts. None of us. We tried to delve into our past with dream interpretation, during the last half of our flight, but we just don't know who we were before we started training. We just get a few flashbacks during deep sleep. What happened to us? Is there any way for us to remember our pasts? Over."

Another six minutes passed, Louis answered, and after six transmission minutes more, Brother Mark heard:

"Yes, everyone is dying, all over the planet. I am lucky to have locked myself into this building and saw it on the newscasts before they stopped broadcasting, weeks ago. And it's not just the Covid War we are losing, it is the Climate Change War. And, thanks to Chinese expansionism and Russian offensiveness, and worldwide cyberterrorism, we are losing the War on War. Now nothing works. There is no television, no radio, no internet, no phones, no banks, no hospitals, no doctors or nurses, no transportation system. No busses, trains, planes, or even bicycles or motorcycles. Nobody is on the streets in metropolitan areas or small towns, except for dead bodies. There may be people who have not yet been affected, due to remoteness, like the military on submarines and possibly some remote primitive islands, but there is no way to know for sure. It is too dangerous to even walk in the streets. Just the slightest exposure to a living person with the virus, even dead people or pets, and you die. I raided vending machines throughout this building, but I am soon to run out of food and water..

"As for your other question, regarding your memories, yes, they were buried by hypno. I alone am able to undo it for you three, with one word. and the word is 'abracadabra'. With that word, all three of you should be able to break out of the hypno, and regenerate your memories; just keep repeating that word to yourselves and yo each other. I will help if you need it, that is, as long as I am still alive. Louis, over."

Brother Mark could barely believe what he was hearing, but, having heard '"adracadabra", he suddenly began to retrieve memories from deep within his brain. Neurotransmitters came alive, and his memories began to break out. It was like a lifting fog, revealing a clear world, and as if he was surrounded by frosted glass which suddenly shattered to expose fact and truth. He, now he knew his real name, "Jim Long", and his young Chinese-American wife, Anna, had been scientists. She had been sent to China, in 2019 to Wuhan Virus Laboratory, to transport a lunar rock from the Apollo program, stored for decades at UA, to the Chinese laboratory for virology analysis. His daughter Susie travelled with his wife to China. His wife Anna died in China and her ashes were returned to the United States with his daughter, who also died of a virus infection while on the return aircraft. Many on the aircraft became also ill with what later was found to be Covid-19. Unknowingly the passengers on that flight went about their lives and spread the virus among their families and friends. Eventually, as viruses do, Covid-19 formed variants, and those variants formed variants. The variant that Louis was referring to was originally Covid-19, but it mutated and gradually necame "The Andromeda Variant".

The six minute transmission period passed and Brother Mark (Jim now), just stood by the communication panel and had not told the two Sisters yet, but time ticked quickly as he sorted things out and he felt he had to respond.

"I think you are saying that my wife and daughter were the originators of Covid-19, which now has mutated, and the mutations have mutated, to the Andromeda variant, which will destroy humanity on Earth. Is that right? My God, that makes me feel my family is to blame for the extinction of the human race on Earth. MarsX over."

He then went to the Sisters and told them the magic word and said they should just repeat it to each other for awhile. They too felt the lifting of fog and the breaking of frosted glass, and began to remember who they really were before they started training. Jim returned to the communication panel.

Time passed, and Louis replied:

"No. The cause of the virus getting out was the poor safety handling of the moonrock by the Chinese laboratory. I suppose you could say that the root cause was the moonrock, itself, or bringing it to Earth. Some people feel that to hold a rock from the Moon is like touching the hand of God. Your wife just happened to be in the wrong place at the wrong time with the wrong person. She simply transported the moonrock for analysis under totally safe conditions, and it was under strict safety protocol from the time it was picked up on the Moon by astronauts and while it was stored at U of A for fifty-some years, until it was in the hands of the Chinese laboratory. Your daughter was obviously not doing anything wrong either, although in hindsight, nobody should have been allowed to board that plane. It has been kept a national secret all this time for political purposes and I am not even supposed to tell you, but under the circumstances, I see no problem with that. Louis, over"

Brother Mark went back to the craft and discussed the "word" with the two Sisters. Sister Martha was now Gertrude, and Sister Margie was now Elizabeth. "Jim" reintroduced himself to them, and they all worked for a few minutes to reaquaint themselves with their new identities and memories in the MarsX expedition. Jim returned to the panel, his mind racing between past and future, just in time to speak to Louis:

"Now, Louis, with what you have told me, we don't have much to do here any more...our mission is pointless. If Earth society is gone, as you are saying, then there is little to gain from the artifacts and coins here on Mars. We could gather up coins for the rest of our lives here on Mars and it would never be possible to ever return them to Earth and even if we did, there would be no one to deal with them intellectualy. We need to rethink our "mission".

I completely forgot to tell you about our Martian friend, Adamus. He is a young, ambitious Martian man who wants more than anything to go to Earth, and we are probably going to work on that for awhile. We are thinking that we might send him, using the ten percent of our rocket fuel remaining, and a small portion of our craft. Sister Margie, (Elizabeth), can help us to achieve that. MarsX over."

In time, Louis responded: "That objective sounds good, but if you do succeed in overcoming the transport difficuty, you should send him and a female to a very remote and desolate place on this planet.

I suppose that would be somewhere like an uninhabited island in Micronesia or Polynesia or possibly the North Pole or Antartica. Any place with a population that has any connections with the modern world would result in death from the Andromeda variant.

We may lose our connection in a few minutes due to rotation of the planets. If so, I wish to express my sincere jubilation in hearing from you, that you are well. I suggest we attempt at same time tomorrow. Control Over."

7

ARTH RETURN

Jim returned to the craft and told the two other astronauts what he had heard from Louis and what he had told Louis. The three conversed hyperactively for awhile and Jim realized that they were all having problems with keeping their minds straight and focused. He also felt that the information was too shocking to understand without deep thinking. So he suggested that they all quietly meditate on their cots for awhile to clear their minds. Gertrude and Elizabeth were in total agreement and they had a bit to eat from the goodies Louis had brought, and then went to meditate on their cots.

After some time, Adamus came to the craft on his gorth. He tapped on the door with a rock and Gertrude, although in deep meditative state, heard the tapping and went to open the door. Adamus was talking but she could not hear, so she put her hand on the floor next to him and he climbed into it. She carried him to the table with microphone as Brother Mark (Jim) had done before. Adamus said:

"I see you have another craft located nearby. Is it supplies, food and water?"

"No", said Gerturde, "It is a communication device for talking with Control on Earth."

Adamus replied, "Oh good, I hope you were able to use it and get some latest information and to inform them of your status." He continued, "I have brought you more of the gorth food in bags which are on my gorth. Please help me to bring it into your craft. I did not bring you gorths for another expedition to the crater because I thought you would like to do it on another day."

By that time Jim, hearing Adamus' voice on the speakers, had come out of his meditative state and joined them at the table. "Adamus," he said, "we have regained communication from our Control on Earth, using equipment that we received yesterday. We received some very distressing news. There is a virus that is killing all of the people on Earth. It was bad when we left but now it is worse. it is destroying humanity on Earth. It is spread through human to human contact, and now it has mutated to a point where it is no longer under control."

"How horrible!" said Adamus. "We have similar viruses on our planet. but we control trem with masks. By simply wearing masks, we prevent the spread of the disease from one to another. We also avoid contact with each other as much as we can, no touching or kissing or hugging allowed. But our scientists do warn us about a deadly kind of virus that could happen in the future, that may find a way to defeat our practices."

"Yes, we have had similar anti-virus practices on Earth for many years. But now the virus has mutated to a point where we seem helpless to prevent its spread. My wife and child died from an earlier virus mutation. It possibly came from a rock brought back from Earth's Moon."

"I'm very sorry," said Adamus.

Jim went on,

"Now humanity is dying, on Earth, from a virus. We no longer have a mission here on Mars. There is no point to search for ancient artifacts here, they are useless. I am thinking now that we may try to return to Earth with our craft. Time is of the essense, because every day the distance from Mars to Earth becomes a million miles greater. Here is a sketch of my idea so far:

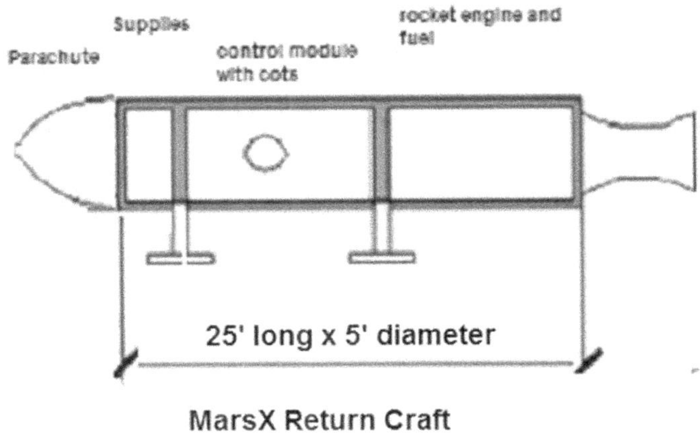

MarsX Return Craft

"You see, we can simply remove two of the sections, the R&R and the sleep section. This will allow us to cut down almost half of our payload weight. With the smaller gravity on Mars, and the 'downhill' fall from Mars to Earth, we may be able to get home with our remaining fuel. Sister Margie, uh, Gertrude, can hopefully verify that with calculations. The only problem I can see is that we need to do some cutting and welding and lifting. Is there any possiblity that you can help with that?"

Adamus replied: "I believe I can help you. Perhaps with some of that brandy that we tried a few days ago, we can persuade some of my friends to work on it. I'll have to do some asking around. I happen to know a welder, an electrician, and a guy with a grinder, and a big guy who does lifting. You have electric power on this craft, right?"

Jim said, "Yes, we get solar powered batteries from our solar panels, for cooking and heating. Fortunately we received some more liquer bottles from our boss, they were packed with the communication device."

Adamus: "Do you think I could return to Arth with you? It has been my life-long dream. Ivanka and I have been together for a long time and I think I must bring her with me. I think she would."

Jim: "I see no problem with that. We would need to train you about the many things necessary for the trip. It is a long trip, and will take over 60 sols. You will need to be very, very patient during the voyage. There is weightlessness issue. Also food and water issue. But we can probably work them out."

Adamus: "Fine with me, put me back on my gorth and I will do some looking around for help with the craft."

Jim, "Certainly."

He took Adamus back to the doorway of the craft. Adamus signaled to his gorth, mounted it, and was off.

Jim turned to face Gertrude and Elizabeth. They both said at the same time, as if Siamese twins attached at the waist, "We're going home?"

Jim: "If we can. What do you think? Our mission here is no longer valid."

Gertrude: "I'll check into the power need to return home, payload will be crucial."

Elizabeth: "I'll check into a landing site on Earth. Like Louis suggested, we need to look at remote and uninhabited islands."

Jim: "I will work on gathering and drying kelp for the trip. Also water."

With that they all focused on their tasks for most of the day. Near sundown, they regrouped.

Gertrude said: "It looks feasible. We will need half our remaining fuel to get into orbit, and a quarter more to get out of orbit, and what's left to decelerate when we get to Earth. But that is with half our original payload."

Elizabeth then reviewed her study: "There are thousands of uninhabited islands on Earth. I looked at what I am a little familiar with. In Micronesia, there was Bikini Island, used as an atomic bomb test site long ago. They tried to locate some of the original inhabitants back to it but they all started to develop radiation poisoning from the underground well water and the seafood. Likewise for a nearby island. Then there is an island off of San Francisco, Farallon Island. It has no vegetation and the military dumped 47,500 nuclear waste drums in the ocean offshore, which are leaking and polluting all the surrounding sea life. There's no water except seasonal rain. Then there is Alcatraz Island in San Francisco Bay, uninhabited now, but again, no water source. There are uninhabited islands in the Alutian Island chain, at the western end of the chain, that have vegetation and probably well water, but winters and storms are pretty severe, and there is an active volcano spewing ash all over the island. Also there is an uninhabited atoll in the South Pacific where they found signs of Amelia Earhart's plane in 2021, Nikamaroro. That seems like it has vegetation and well water, people have lived there from time to time, but the problem I see is that it has cyclones, Pacific Ocean equivalent of Atlantic hurricanes, occasionally, which sometimes flood the island.

"So that's about as far as I got, I guess there may be other places around the world, I need to do more research about. Galapagos Islands, for example...I am looking for islands that are remote, uninhabited, with vegetation and water, livable, temperate climate, and safe."

Jim: "I collected enough kelp and water for about a week but I'll keep working on that. We will need about ten weeks for the trip. Adamus will have to get us about a hundred pounds of gorth food."

With that, and sunset upon them, they all retired for the evening in their cots.

Sol 5, (February 23, 2027)

In the morning, after sunshine warmed the air, Jim plodded to the communication panel and contacted Louis, as planned. Louis was there, waiting for the call. Jim informed Louis of their plans to return to Earth as soon as possible. They would try to use the second panel to replace the broken parts on the old panel, so that they could keep in touch during the trip. Louis had found some food stored in the building so he was good for awhile.

Louis said that it seemed better than the way he had explained the day before...he now sees that there could be some survivors, such as on the Moon and the International Space Station, and astronauts that are in transit. In addition he had heard some short-wave activity on his own radio receiver from people who had isolated themselves from the virus in underground shelters, with their families. And, there were probably isolated small groups of islanders around the world who had saved themselves on small, remote islands around the world.

Jim remarked that it appeared humanity may survive the virus, barely, but it will have to wait awhile for the virus to die out before it will be safe for humans to mix socially, probably for years.

Louis asked, "So how long will it be before you leave Mars."

Jim responded, " It depends on how long it takes to cut our payload down. We have not heard yet from our Martian who is looking into that."

Louis; "We need to end our communication now until tomorrow morning. Louis, over and out."

Jim: "Over and out."

As he said that Jim looked up and could see Adamus arriving with several other people, all of different size. Adamus was leading them and came directly to Jim at the comm panel.

Adamus: "Good morning, Jim. I have brought some of my Martian friends. There is one guy to do the cutting, one to do the electrial wiring, one to do the welding, and one for lifting."

Jim; "Wonderful. We need to proceed immediately as time is of the essence." Please direct them and get it all going as quickly as possible."

Adamus turned to his several people and yelled with a megaphone to them in Marstalk. They all understood exactly what to do. They all entered the craft except the very large "lifter", who stayed outside, up to his chest in sand. The cutter, from inside the R&R section, began cutting with an electric circular saw and thin grindstone. He proceeded to cut around the entire R&R section within a short time, and then proceeded to do the same in the Supply section and then in the Control section. Then the lifter took out the two cut-away sections and placed them on the sand next to the craft. He moved the Control section next to the rocket portion and then put the supply section next to the Control Section. The electrician had been studying the wiring all the time they were working, and the welder began to weld the sections together right away. The electrician put the wiring together as it was originally, wire by wire, and the new craft was pretty much ready to go, with close to half them original payload as it was for the original liftoff. They needed to replace the parachute in the nose cone and set the cots on the Control section walls. By day's end the entire job was completed, except for the food and water supplies.

Jim, Gertrude, and Elizabeth stood around, watching the incredibly fast work that occurred, and gave the workers most of the liquer, thanking them for their work as they left for home near the end of the day.

Adamus left as well, and said he will be back in the morning with more gorth food. The astronauts ate, drank, and retired to their new cots.

Sol 6, (February 24, 2027)

As he did the day before, Jim contacted Louis and gave him an update. He was actually able to photograph the craft in it's new revised condition and transmit the photo to Louis. Louis was astounded and exclaimed, "You are nearly ready to launch! Unbelievable"

Jim: "Yes, Louis, I am also amazed and excited that we may be ready to leave as soon as our food and water supply is adequate. I will contact you in the morning. Jim, over and out."

Louis, "Over and out."

Sol 7, (February 25, 2027)

Adamus showed up early in the morning. He brought a lot of gorth food. There was clearly sufficient for the trip.

Jim called Louis right away and notified him that they were

almost ready. They were capable to leave very soon, but needed to check out the controls and see that everything is in place. Gertrude spent the morning studying the gauges, lights, and switches on the control panel. Elizabeth saw that the food and water were placed in the Supply section of the craft. Jim prepared the drinking water by filtering the water that he got from soaking it up with rags from the sand below.

Ivanka came on a gorth soon after mid-sol, and Elizabeth saw that she was tied down with Adamus under a strap on the table. She was followed by a whole bunch of gorths full of people from the community, including the relatives of Adamus and Ivanka. Jim saw the gorths, surrounding the craft in a large circle, and then he told the travellers, "We are ready for lift-off."

Adamus and Ivanka said they were ready. Jim sealed the door tightly and the three astronauts strapped themselves into their seats in the crowded Control section. Gertrude began a countdown. "Ten, nine, eight..." She used the retro rockets to upright the craft and ignited the rocket engine.

They arced into the sky and then orbited the "red planet" one time only, and then fired the rocket engine again to put them on a trajectory for a 60-sol trip. Gertrude had set up a way to manufacture oxygen using the batteries, charged by solar cells, and hydrolosis, so the cabin oxygen level slowly increased as they travelled, to match that on their destination.

Sixty days later, they arrived at the "blue planet", decelerated, orbited the planet once, and finally landed on the white beach next to the blue lagoon of Nikamororo Island.

Lightning Source UK Ltd.
Milton Keynes UK
UKHW011826180522
403172UK00001B/114